The Third Base Coach

A Ricky Temple PI Story

Book 2

By Joe Quigley

Other Ricky Temple PI stories:

Trouble in Beer City

The Third Base Coach

First paperback and digital editions published in 2025
by Kindle Direct Publishing

This is a work of fiction.
Although a few characters are based on friends of the author,
the majority are from the author's imagination just like the story itself.
Some locations are real, some location names
were slightly changed for fun.
It's entertainment.

Cover design and formatting by Amy J. West
with resources from Canva, DinosoftLabs from Flatiron, Lee Gordon, Nick's Fonts, and iStockphoto (ca2hill and Tina Zimmer).

Contact joe@joequigleyauthor.com
or visit www.joequigleyauthor.com for further information.

Paperback ISBN 979-8-218-85323-5

Dedication

For my wife. Not only does she get to hear about my ideas constantly, but she also inspired the character, Susan. Thank you.

To my old Army buddy Pink who inspired the character RJ Floyd, thank you.

Father Christian Cook, my lifelong friend who inspired Father Tim Daniels, thank you.

Contents

Some of my fondest memories of my college days were playing intramural sports with my fraternity brothers. We didn't always have the best teams, but we had a lot of fun. We took it seriously, most of the time, and I never understood why we got up at 8 a.m. on Saturday mornings for basketball practice. In the story you are about to read, I took the liberty of using some of their nicknames or partial names as a way of thanking them for such great times. I am disappointed I couldn't use all of them. There just weren't enough characters in the story.

To all the guys from those years, I hope it brings back good memories for you. I still look back on those days and smile.

Chapter 1

After another lap around his office, Tommy Bonetti settled in behind his desk, still annoyed.

"Those guys should have been here two hours ago," he yelled at anyone who would listen, "They've been late the last two trips. How hard is it? All they have to do is put the suitcases with the money in the car, get on I-85 North in Atlanta and drive until they get to North Main Street here in High Point, North Carolina. It's not that hard. But every month it's the same thing."

"Aren't they coming from Newark this time? I know how frustrated you get with them, and I talked to them the last time," Gina said. "How much are they bringing, and are they bringing any product?"

"Same as last, $500K and no product, that's coming later. I wish they were bringing some product; I could use some. Everything we have needs to be sold. They came from Newark last time, so this trip is from Atlanta. If they aren't here soon, I'm going to have to leave to go to that meeting over at Sully's Irish Pub," he said.

"Go ahead to your meeting. I'll take care of the money until you get back," Gina said.

"Okay, I need to get to the meeting. Remind these two they have to stay here for a couple of weeks while we figure out the money distribution. Maybe they will sell some tires this time."

Tommy walked out of Tommy's Tire Emporium, the store he and Gina opened over 25 years ago. As he walked to his car, he saw a car with a Georgia license plate pull into the parking lot.

"I don't have time to yell at you guys. Pull the car into one of the bays and unload the suitcases. We sent the other employees to lunch, so they won't see anything. Gina is inside waiting for you. Make sure you are here when I get back," Tommy said.

It was the last day of Susan Temple's contract at the U.S. Naval Academy Museum and Ricky was waiting for her to finish her out briefing. He was happy when the front door opened, and Susan came out ready to head to Baltimore. With a big smile, she said, "Are you ready for some baseball?"

"Opening day. We still have a chance at the playoffs," Ricky said as they started toward the walk-in gate of the Academy. They walked past the guard manning the check point and crossed King George Street onto the sidewalk of Maryland Avenue. Eventually, they found themselves in front of Galway Bay Irish Pub where they had dinner a few times over the last couple of weeks.

"That reminds me, will we have time to eat before the game?" Susan asked.

"Of course, it's only about 45 minutes to Camden Yards and the game doesn't start until 1:00 p.m. I just want to be in the stadium in time to see the opening day ceremonies."

After another few minutes of walking they arrived at the parking garage, ready to brave the drive from Annapolis to Baltimore.

Less than an hour later, Ricky and Susan pulled into a parking lot close to the stadium. Ricky found a parking spot he thought would be easy to get out of when the game was over. When they had gathered what they needed, he intentionally walked around the stadium to get a look at Pickles Pub, across from the ballpark. He knew better than to go in there since he was wearing his beloved

Red Sox jersey and hat, so he and Susan opted for Boog Powells BBQ for lunch.

It was a big day and Ricky was excited. He had never been to opening day before.

Tommy drove the few blocks to Sully's Irish Pub. He parked illegally, like he always does.

He walked into the Pub and saw the group he was there to meet in a back corner. He found a seat as far away from Johnny Sullivan as he could. He hated Johnny.

"Great, I think everyone is here. Just to be sure, let me call off all the names. Tommy from Tommy's Tire Emporium just arrived. Tiny from Tiny's Auto Supply and Towing and Les Tucker from Tucker's Paint and Drywall. Of course, Johnny Sullivan is here since he was nice enough to let us meet at his place, Sully's Irish Pub. Okay, good. As a reminder, I am Mike Kinney the commissioner of our league which is part of the North Carolina Adult Coed Softball Association. Welcome to the new spring season," Mike said, addressing everyone but only getting blank stares.

"I don't see why we have to meet here!" Tommy yelled.

"I guess you would rather meet at your tire store, I'm sorry, *emporium*, so we can all sit on tires for this meeting. That's classy!" Johnny yelled back at his rival.

Last season the league championship came down to Tommy's Tires and Sully's Irish Pub. There was bad blood between the two teams the entire season and several cheap shots from both teams didn't help matters. It also didn't help that Tommy and Gina like to frequent Sully's and have been thrown out a few times for making a scene. Most people thought there was more to it than a softball rivalry.

"Gentlemen, let's get back to business. I'm interested in kicking off the spring season and nothing else today," Mike said, regaining control of the meeting.

"As you all may have heard, this year the winner of our league will advance to the regional finals in Greensboro, and the winner will go to the final four with a chance at a championship in Asheville early this summer. Games start next week, and each of you will receive this year's schedule later today or tomorrow morning. Are there any questions?" Mike asked.

"Yes, I have one," Les Tucker said. Les moved to High Point several years ago after he burned out being a radio personality in Cincinnati. He loved softball and played for his radio station team back in Cincinnati. "Have any of the rules changed? Can we steal bases this year?"

"No changes to the rules. You know we follow the state rules to ensure we can be eligible for the state tournament," Mike answered. "So, no stealing or bunting. If a pitch hits a batter, then it's called a ball. Anything else?"

Tiny raised his hand. Tiny was a respected business owner who lived in High Point his entire life. The city uses his towing service for illegally parked cars. "Is there a maximum number of players and coaches this year? Last year we could have a total of 14 per team and had to let you know if someone got hurt so we could replace them."

"Same this year. No changes there either. If there are no other questions, we can end the meeting so you can all get back to work. Let's have a good season and keep it clean so nobody gets hurt.

Remember, this is supposed to be fun," Mike said, ending the meeting.

"He's talking to you, Tommy. You'd better hope nobody on your team slides into my knees again this year!" Johnny yelled.

"You worry about your team, and I'll worry about mine," Tommy said, walking out. He had more important things to do than getting into a yelling match with Johnny Sullivan.

After they had all gone, Johnny walked over to the bar where Riley Simms was setting up for the day. She has been the main bartender at Sully's for the last three years after graduating from Charlotte, where she pitched on the softball team.

"I guess you heard all that. Tommy Bonetti is a jackass. Can you call and check on the uniforms for this year while I call the team to set up a practice for later this week? Also, I'm thinking about bringing in a third base coach to help me keep an eye on Tommy's Tires, I just don't trust him," Johnny said.

"No problem, I'll check on the uniforms and will let you know," Riley replied.

Ricky's phone rang as he and Susan walked out of Camden Yards. He was feeling dejected since the Sox dropped the season opener. *Not a good start to the season*, he thought.

"Hey Johnny, what's going on? Everything okay in the neighborhood?" Ricky asked, answering the phone.

Johnny Sullivan, the owner of Sully's Irish Pub, had gone to college in nearby Greensboro. After getting his undergraduate degree in business, he stayed and got his master's degree as well. He fell in love with the area and stayed to open the pub with his friend. Eventually Johnny bought him out and became the sole owner of Sully's Irish Pub. Over the years he made a lot of friends in High Point, including Ricky and Susan Temple.

Ricky and Susan lived near Johnny, just north of downtown High Point. When Ricky and Susan started frequenting Sully's Pub, they became friends and learned they lived close to each other.

"Yeah, everything is fine. I went by your condo yesterday and didn't see anything to worry about. When do you get back from Baltimore?" Johnny asked.

"We should be back in High Point by midafternoon tomorrow. Do you need something?"

"Yeah, can you stop by the bar tomorrow evening? There's something I want to talk to you about," Johnny said.

"Sure, sounds good. I'll be there after we get settled," Ricky said. *Click.*

"What was that about?" Susan asked.

"Johnny wants me to drop by the pub tomorrow night. He wants to talk about something."

"Is it PI stuff?" she asked.

"Not sure, and you know it's private investigator," he said.

After a nice dinner at G&M Restaurant for the best crab cakes around, Ricky and Susan went back to the hotel to pack for the trip home. They had been away from home for three weeks, a week in France and two weeks in Annapolis, so they had a few bags to go through.

The next morning at Baltimore International Airport, Ricky sat at the gate while Susan went to the bathroom. She got back just as their flight was finally called.

"Well then, shall we go?" Susan said sliding her arm into his.

"We shall," he responded. They both chuckled.

Once onboard, Ricky pulled out his noise cancelling headphones and plugged them in so he could listen to the 80's satellite station. Susan was getting situated when she heard him. Ricky was singing as loud as he could, pretty much screaming. He had no idea how loud it was because of his noise cancelling headphones.

Susan sat there, embarrassed. Not only was he singing very loudly, but he was also off key and didn't know all the words. She turned toward him and got his attention. "You're singing really loud," she said.

"THANKS. IT'S ETERNAL FLAME BY THE BANGLES. WHAT A GREAT SONG," he said, and went back to singing.

Susan dropped her head into her hands. She finally reached over and unplugged his headphones. "You are yelling, not singing. Everyone can hear you sing off key, and you don't even know the words!"

Ricky looked around the plane. Several rows of people stared at him. Someone started clapping for him, and most of the other passengers joined in, clapping and cheering.

"Thanks, I'll be with you for the next hour and a half," Ricky announced. He put his headphones back on and mouthed the words, never getting loud enough for anyone to hear for the rest of the flight.

By 2:00 p.m. they were at their condo and unpacking. Ricky wondered what Johnny wanted to talk to him about.

Chapter 2

A little after 7:00 p.m., Ricky pulled into the parking lot across the street from Sully's Irish Pub. He parked, waited for a few cars to pass, and then crossed the street. As he walked into the pub, he looked around to see who was there. As usual it was dark and about half full. He saw Riley behind the bar and Juice and Gravy from Johnny's softball team throwing darts in the corner.

Ricky thought it was a good crowd for a Wednesday night, and he was always happy when they played Dropkick Murphys. It was an Irish pub, after all. He waved to Riley and walked over.

"Before you start in on me, I don't want to hear any crap tonight. I'm in a bad mood," Riley said. "My boyfriend dumped me this morning."

"Boyfriend? I didn't know you had a boyfriend. Sorry it didn't work out. How long were you two together?" Ricky asked.

"A week and a half," she said.

"Oh. Okay. I'll take a Miller High Life," Ricky said.

"Didn't I just tell you to not mess with me tonight? I've worked here for three years and during that time you have come in a few times a week ordering Miller High Life. You know we don't have it. Then tonight I tell you not to start with me and you do it anyway!" Riley yelled at Ricky.

"It's the champagne of beer," Ricky said.

"I don't care if it's the champagne of champagne. We don't carry it, and you know it," Riley said. "One of these days you are going to come in, and I won't be here. I am going to move to the Caribbean. There are about 30 inhabitable islands, I just need to pick one."

"I know, you've told me this before. Back to my beer, how about Sam Adams Boston Lager?"

"So, your usual, Sam Boston," she replied.

"Oh, hey Riley, do you know what a hot mess is?" Ricky asked with a smirk. He loved to get her riled up.

Riley gave him an annoyed look and said, "I do and I'm not one."

She reached into the cooler and pulled out a Sam Boston, took the top off, and put it in front of Ricky. After staring at each other for a few seconds, they both laughed. It was their usual banter. If someone didn't know better, they'd think they didn't like each other. Riley liked Ricky and Susan and considered them friends as well as some of her favorite customers.

"Who's the new waitress? I haven't seen her before," Ricky asked, changing the subject.

"Oh, her. That's Samantha. She started a few days ago. Not a bad waitress, I guess."

"It doesn't sound like you care for her too much," Ricky said.

"She's okay, but she is a big Taylor Swift fan. All day it's Tay Tay this and Tay Tay that. She asks several times a day why we don't play Taylor Swift. So annoying. Oh, it's almost time for the toast. Do you want your usual, Powers Gold Label Irish Whiskey?"

"Yeah, that sounds good, thanks. Where is Johnny? He called me yesterday and wanted me to drop by."

"He's in the back. Ever since he got distracted doing the toast a few weeks ago, he set up a microphone in his office so he can do it from there."

Abruptly the Dropkick Murphys song stopped, and Johnny Sullivan's voice came over the sound system.

"Good evening, Sully's Irish Pub!" Johnny said to some cheers. "If you've been here before, then you know what time it is. The clock says it's 7:33 p.m., but at Sully's we do the 24-hour clock. That means it's 1933 and we all know what happened in 1933, right?" Johnny was getting excited now.

Regulars at the pub cheered while some new customers looked confused.

"Repeal the 18th!" yelled one person.

"Down with Prohibition!" said another.

"No taxation without representation!" chimed in a third, clearly not understanding what was happening.

Chewey, another member of the softball team, turned to someone who looked confused and said, "If you think this is crazy, you should be here on December 5th, the actual day prohibition ended. The final three states needed to overturn prohibition ratified the 21st Amendment on that day. It started in the afternoon with Pennsylvania and Ohio. Then at 3:52 p.m. mountain time, Utah approved the amendment. A few minutes later the Undersecretary of State signed it. So, on December 5th there are multiple toasts and parties. That's a crazy day and I never miss it."

"We have a tradition here at Sully's because the year 1933 had a significant event. Raise your glass and toast the end of prohibition," Johnny continued. Even with the office door closed, he could hear the cheers. Johnny thought they were louder than usual tonight, so he paused an extra few seconds before going on.

"And now, we ask that everyone rise, and gentlemen, we use the term gentlemen loosely around here, please remove your caps for the playing of our national anthem," Johnny said. He turned off his microphone and pushed play. He sat back in his chair and took a breath.

When the national anthem was done, Ricky put his now empty glass on the bar. He knew Riley would be busy for a while refilling the glasses that were just emptied. He looked at her and pointed toward the office. She nodded and gave him a thumbs up.

Ricky walked down the short hallway past the bathrooms to the office door. He knocked before walking in. Johnny had a small office with enough room for a desk with his laptop on it and a chair for one visitor.

"Good toast tonight," Ricky said from the door.

"Ricky T, thanks. Come on in. How was Baltimore?"

"As you probably saw, the Sox lost. The starting pitching still looks bad, but we will see how the season plays out. We had some good food, so it wasn't a total loss. What's up?" Ricky asked.

"Thanks for coming in. I knew you would be in sooner rather than later. I wanted to talk to you about the pub's softball team," Johnny said.

Ricky perked up when he heard that. He had been wanting to get on the team for some time. "Okay, what do you have in mind?" Ricky asked.

"You know in past years we had some problems with another team?"

"You're talking about Tommy's Tire Emporium. I was at the game when Otis threw the ball at Tommy's head instead of to first base. I was also at the game when Gina Bonetti kept trying to hit Riley," Ricky said.

"Were you here for the season Tommy bought an old firetruck and his team rode it to all the games?"

"I heard about it. There was a rumor that Tiny used one of his trucks to tow it away after the last game," Ricky said.

"That's a true story. I was pulling into the parking lot when it was leaving," Johnny said.

"Do Tommy and Gina still drink here?" Ricky asked.

"They come in, but not as much as before. I haven't had to throw them out in a long time. I don't mind if they drink here, as long as they don't cause any problems. Don't get me wrong, I don't get any discount on tires, and they don't get any drinks on the house," Johnny said.

"Where do I fit into all this?" Ricky asked.

"We had the preseason managers' meeting a couple of days ago. It doesn't look like things have calmed down between Tommy and us. It might be worse for some reason. I was hoping you could join the team and help me keep an eye on it. With all your PI and military experience, I think you could keep it calm or help if something goes crazy. What do you think?" Johnny asked.

"It's private investigator. So, you want to hire me?" Ricky asked, winking at his friend.

"I was thinking you would join the team and get a feel for what's going on. If there is something to investigate, then yes, I would hire you to take care of it," Johnny responded. "If I hire you, maybe we could exchange your bar tab for your services."

"Any thoughts on why there is so much tension between you and Tommy?" Ricky asked.

"Like we already talked about, he and Gina come in and drink too much sometimes and I have to kick them out. Plus, the softball league championship has come down to our teams in the last few years, so maybe he holds that against me. I guess it might not have helped that I gave his business a bad review one time. I don't know. There is just some edge to Tommy that I can't figure out. He is always worked up," Johnny said.

"I've never been to his tire store. I always just assumed it was somewhat successful since they've been around so long. Interesting situation, we have a deal," Ricky said. He reached over the desk to shake Johnny's hand. "Tell me about the team."

"You know most of the team. A lot of them spend time here in the pub after work and are probably out there now. You already mentioned Otis and there is Woody, Juice, Gravy, Caldwell, Chewey, and Joe B. Obviously, I play and Riley pitches for us. We have practice tomorrow at 6:00 p.m. Our first game is next Tuesday at 7:00 against Tiny's Auto Supply and Towing. Can you make practice tomorrow night?"

"Yeah, that's no problem. I'll tell you what, I will pick you up here on the way," Ricky suggested.

"That will work. I think you already know, but after practice and games we all come back here and have a couple of beers and hang out. We have a rotation of two people that stay after practice and get all the bats and balls gathered up while everyone heads here. Then they come over after cleaning up and join us. It's part of being on the team," Johnny explained.

"I like it. I'll be here about 5:30 to get you," Ricky said, standing to leave.

Ricky walked back to the bar. He ordered another Sam Boston and took out his phone to call Susan.

"Hey, I just talked to Johnny. He wants me on the softball team. There's still a lot of tension between Johnny and Tommy Bonetti. He wants me around to keep an eye on things," Ricky said.

"So, it's a job?" she asked.

"Not yet. If anything develops then he wants me to take care of it. If that happens, we are going to exchange my services for our bar tab. I'll be home soon. I need to find all my baseball gear. I'll probably be playing a lot so you might want to free up some time to come see me in action."

"Yes dear," she said.

When Ricky got home, he went through all his storage containers in the garage and then moved on to the attic to find his stuff. Two hours later he finally found his baseball glove. An hour after that he found his cleats, but they didn't fit.

"That's okay. I'll just go to the sporting goods store tomorrow morning and buy new ones," Ricky said.

"You mean, you'll go buy new ones after you clean this mess up and put everything back where it was before you tore it all out?" Susan said, looking at Ricky over the top of her glasses. It was more a statement than a question.

"That's exactly what I meant. Then I'll stretch out and get my arm ready," he said.

"Okay, can we go to sleep now? I tried to go to sleep an hour ago, but you were making all kinds of noise. I'm tired," she said.

"Of course. No problem," Ricky said.

Ricky had been asleep for a short time when he suddenly jerked up out of bed in a panic. He couldn't breathe and his heart was racing. He tried to gather himself before going into the living room to turn the TV on. He needed to have some light. The bedroom was just too dark when he had these dreams.

Ricky was watching TV when Susan came in.

"Are you okay?" she asked.

"I had another dream. This time I was scuba diving, looking at all these fish, when suddenly I was stuck in the water, and everything went black. I couldn't breathe or move. It was as if the water had become concrete. I didn't have any air. That's when I woke up.

The darkness is hard for me when these dreams happen," he explained.

"Remember when we were working in Asheville, you promised RJ you would go see someone about this? You never did. I'm going to make some calls and find someone for you to see," Susan said. She was worried about him especially since the dreams had been coming more frequently. Susan didn't wait for a response and stood up and went back to bed.

The next morning, after Ricky finished his coffee, he started putting the house back together. He was tired, which he didn't like because he had softball practice later. Ricky stacked the last box in the garage when Susan came in.

"You have an appointment next Wednesday at 10:00 a.m. to see Dr. B. F. Pearce. I talked to his nurse or receptionist, not sure which. She was nice, and I told her a little bit about the situation," Susan said, not sure how he would respond.

Ricky forced a smile and said, "Okay, thanks." He walked into the living room, got the car keys, and went to the sporting goods store.

Tommy stopped at the screen printer on his way to the tire store to make sure his team's uniforms were correct. It wouldn't be the first time a number was wrong, or a name was misspelled. So, at the start of every season, he goes by and checks. After that, he went to work.

Jason and Neil, the couriers who brought the suitcases of money up from Atlanta, were pretending to be tire salesmen. At first glance, anyone who walked in would think that's exactly what they were. If anyone looked closely, they might notice they were both carrying guns, but nobody would see the two automatic rifles under the counter. The couriers were Tommy and Gina's first line of defense for what was stored in the back. He hoped they were good security guards because they were terrible tire salesmen.

Tommy walked past them, said hello, and went straight to the office. Gina was there waiting for him. They were both on edge today because a new shipment was due anytime now. It wouldn't be money this time.

"I talked to Atlanta, those hacker houses they set up brought in a bunch of money again this month," Gina said.

"What are the houses doing? How many do they have now?" Tommy asked.

"They buy people's information on the dark web and send emails and text messages to get people to click on the links. Then they use their information to take out loans in their names or drain their bank accounts. Not sure how many houses they have set up. It's all being run directly from Atlanta. How much are the couriers bringing this time?" Gina asked. Tommy got situated behind his desk.

"50 kilos. I want to get it unloaded and get them out of here as fast as we can. They need to get to Charlotte and then to Athens, Georgia," Tommy replied. "The longer they are here, the greater the chance something will go wrong."

Tommy moved his chair away from his desk and lifted the carpet to reveal the door leading to the storage area under his office. He unlocked it, opened it, and went down the stairs to see what was left of the last shipment. There wasn't much down there but some drugs, or 'product' as they called it. He needed to get the older inventory to his sellers today. He also saw the money Neil and Jason had brought a few days earlier.

A small moving truck with Georgia license plates pulled into the last bay, closest to the office.

"Go ahead and pull in, we'd be happy to check out your tires for you," Tommy said to the driver. He always talked like that when a shipment arrived in case someone was listening. He had no reason to think anyone was, but he wanted it to be second nature.

Thirty minutes later, Tommy's portion of the delivery was unloaded into his secret storage area.

"Good news, I don't see anything wrong with your tires. If something still feels wrong, we have a store in Charlotte too. Feel free to stop back anytime!" Tommy yelled. He made a mental note to get the new product to his sellers as he watched the driver back out of the service bay and leave for his next stop.

Chapter 3

Ricky gave Susan a kiss as he walked out the door for softball practice. "Why are you leaving so early?" Susan asked.

"I have to pick Johnny up at 5:30 p.m. and I don't want to be late," he responded.

"It's only 5:00 and it takes 10 minutes to drive to Sully's from here," Susan said.

"Good point, I need to get going now. First practice!" Ricky yelled, closing the door.

Ricky pulled up in front of Sully's and parked in front of the door. He honked the horn, thinking Johnny would come right out even though he was 15 minutes early.

At 5:25 p.m., Ricky honked the horn again. Johnny came running out and got in. "Anybody else in there need a ride?" Ricky asked.

"No," Johnny replied. "It's Riley's day off. She is probably already at the field with the others warming up."

"Which field are we practicing on today?"

"We have High Point Athletic Park from 6:00 until 7:00. Tommy's Tires has the field after us, so that's when things could get interesting. Keep an eye on things toward the end of practice," Johnny said.

"Okay. Now might be a good time to talk about which position I'll play. I was thinking about shortstop. I was a great shortstop on my college intramural team," Ricky said.

"You aren't playing shortstop," Johnny replied immediately.

"Why? That's my best position."

"Because I play shortstop and it's my team," Johnny said.

"Oh, that makes sense. I can handle any infield position, so whatever you think," Ricky said.

"The infield is pretty well set," Johnny said. "You know Riley played in college, so she pitches. Woody plays first base, Gravy is on second, Caldwell is on third and Juice is the catcher."

"Then where am I going to play?" Ricky asked, not sure he wanted the answer.

"I was thinking you would make a great third base coach. That way you can do what we talked about and keep an eye on things for me. Come on Ricky, think about it, how long ago was college intramural softball? When was the last time you played at all?" Johnny asked.

"I know I'm not as young as I used to be," Ricky said, looking at himself in the rearview mirror. "I guess I do have a touch of grey. It's not like I'm ready to be put in a corner to do paint by numbers though," Ricky replied.

"Come on buddy, I'm not asking you to stand in the corner and do nothing. I just need a good eye on Tommy to head off anything he starts. Can you do that for me?" Johnny asked.

"Of course. Whatever you need," Ricky said as they pulled into the ballfield's parking lot.

They got out of Ricky's car and walked to where the team was warming up. Ricky left his glove in the car and thought, *Getting older sucks.*

"Hey everybody, gather around!" Tommy yelled. "Looks like we have a few minutes while Les Tucker and his team finish their practice. Most of you know Ricky T from the pub. He is joining the team as our third-base coach. He will also be ready to go into the game if someone gets hurt," Johnny said. He added the last part to make Ricky feel a little better.

"Thanks Johnny," Ricky jumped in. "I'm excited to be here and be part of the team. I will start working on signals for us and have them by the next practice. I think we will have one for bunting for sure," he said.

"There's no bunting!" Otis yelled from the back.

"Oh, okay. Then we'll have some signals that don't mean anything, and we will use them to confuse the other teams. The only real one will be for stealing a base," Ricky said.

"There's no stealing bases, either," Joe B. said. Ricky sighed.

"Now that we have that settled, it looks like Les is done. Ricky, you get the infield warmed up. Hit some ground balls to us. Riley, when you are ready let Ricky know and we will start batting practice," Johnny said.

The hour went by fast. Ricky used batting practice to get used to his spot in the third base coach's box. He watched the team hit and run so he would know who had speed and who didn't.

"I thought a softball team was supposed to be here practicing!" someone yelled. Ricky turned around to see it was Tommy Bonetti and some of his team waiting for their turn on the field.

"Come on, get off the field and let a good team practice," Tommy said. He rubbed his nose, making sure there were no signs of the line of cocaine he had just done.

"We'll be done in a few minutes. Then it's all yours," Ricky said.

"What's this, Johnny, you have a new third base coach this year?" Tommy asked. "I don't think that's what your team is lacking. What you need is talent."

"I think we've heard enough. Why don't you just go warm up with your team?" Ricky yelled back.

"I don't need the third base coach from a crap team giving me advice. If I want to stand here and watch, I will. You hear me, third base coach?" Tommy yelled at Ricky.

Ricky turned and walked towards Tommy. The rest of Sully's team followed. Ricky got a few steps from the gate in the chain link fence and stopped. He eyed Tommy Bonetti up and down, realizing it was the first time he had ever been this close to him. He doubted Tommy knew who he was.

Ricky turned around to face the field. "That's probably good for today. Don't you think Johnny?"

"Sounds good, Ricky. Everyone let's head over to the pub. Ricky and I will be the cleanup crew today. We'll see you over there in a few minutes. Riley, get the beers going," Johnny said.

Ricky and Johnny collected the team's equipment. As Ricky walked off the field, he went up to Tommy.

"Nice show you just put on. I hope you enjoyed it because it won't end the same way if you're stupid enough to do it again," Ricky said as he brushed by Tommy Bonetti.

"Johnny had to bring in a PI to coach third base. How cute," Tommy replied.

"It's private investigator and I've heard enough of your shit. Some of these people might be scared of you, but I assure you I am not. Go practice with your team. We are done here. Nice sunglasses," Ricky said. *He does know who I am*, Ricky thought. Tommy was pulled away by some of his teammates.

Ten minutes later, Ricky and Johnny walked into Sully's.

"See what I mean about Tommy?" Johnny asked, taking a swig from his beer.

"Yeah, I see it now. I'm not sure what the problem is, but I want to look into it further. There really isn't a need for all that, it's just a slow pitch softball league. Feels like there is more to it," Ricky said.

"You're on the case and your tab is clean," Johnny said, laughing.

Ricky walked away from the group to call Susan. "I'm finishing up at Sully's. Practice ended badly. I had a run in with Tommy Bonetti. We are officially on the case now. I want to try and understand who he is. Can you dig up what you can on him, and I'll be home soon?"

A couple of hours later, Ricky walked into their condo. Susan was waiting for him.

"So, what position did you get, all-star?" Susan asked.

"Third base coach. Apparently, I'm old. I get it, the rest of the team is in their twenties or early thirties. It's a young man's league," Ricky said. "Tommy started a yelling match as we were finishing practice. Directed most of it at me. He didn't know who I was until Johnny yelled my name. Then he made a comment about me being a PI," Ricky said. "Do you have anything on Tommy Bonetti yet?"

"Yeah, I do. Let me get my computer. I'll be right back," Susan said.

Ricky went outside and sat down. Their condo had a small patio, just big enough for two chairs and a small table. It was a nice night, and Ricky thought the fresh air would help clear his mind.

Susan appeared a few minutes later and handed Ricky a Miller High Life. She knew he wanted to be on the field playing and was putting on a good face to hide his disappointment. She set her Chablis down and got to work.

"Tommy and Gina Bonetti moved here about 25 years ago from Newark, NJ. He had a union job working on the freight docks at the international airport. He worked there for about six years right after high school, when he met Gina. They got married but had a hard time making ends meet, even on his union salary. Gina got a job to help. After a few years, they decided it was too expensive in New Jersey, so they moved to High Point. Soon after they arrived, they opened Tommy's Tire Emporium together. After having some success here, they opened a couple more. One is in Charlotte, and the other is in Athens, Georgia." Susan said.

"I didn't know they had three stores. Any idea where they got the money to finance the first one?" Ricky asked.

"That's where it gets a little weird. I found a bankruptcy filing for them a few years before they moved down here. I haven't found any other income that would support the new business. I have some digging still to do but that should get you started," she told him. She finished her glass of Chablis and went inside.

Susan came back with another round of drinks for each of them and the pizza she had ordered.

"Anything on Gina?" Ricky asked.

"Just that she is from Atlanta and went to a Big 10 school in New Jersey on a softball scholarship. She lost her scholarship after starting fights with the other players on the team. She went on to graduate with a degree in business. I looked at a picture of them on the Tire Emporium website, and I've seen her around town some. Mainly at the grocery store."

"So, they have three tire stores and no money trail to show how they afforded them. I suppose they could have borrowed from family. Or since he was in a union, he could have borrowed from 'The Family,'" Ricky said, using air quotes. "Wait a minute. Remember three or four years ago there was something in the news about the police investigating how money the FBI used in an undercover sting against a crime boss ended up here in High Point?"

"Vaguely, but I'll look into it and see what I can find," Susan said. "Something seems odd. I'll keep looking into it. Do you want to talk about your coaching position? I know you were excited about playing before you left."

"Johnny told me he wanted me to be the third base coach so it would be easier to keep an eye on everything. After the run-in with Tommy after practice, I think I agree with him," Ricky said.

The next day was Johnny's annual BBQ at his house. It was the team's tradition to gather with their families, get their uniforms, and announce the batting order. Johnny liked getting everyone together away from the field for some fun. It was also a chance for the wives and girlfriends to get to know each other.

Ricky and Susan arrived at 1:00 p.m. along with everyone else. Ricky was excited to get his uniform. The jerseys were white with dark green pinstripes, with Sully's Pub written in script at an angle. The hats were green with a white 'S' on the front. Ricky grabbed one and put it on while he waited to get his jersey.

Johnny finally got to Ricky and handed him his jersey with a big smile. Ricky looked at the back to see the number 84 in green. Above the number it said, '3B Coach.'

"I looked it up – 84 is the same number the third base coach for the Red Sox wears. And I left your name off so you could keep a low profile," Johnny said.

"Not sure it matters since Tommy seems to know who I am, but I love it. It's perfect. As they say, it's not about the name on the back of the jersey but the name on the front," Ricky said as he put it on.

With the jerseys handed out, Johnny announced the batting order for the season. "Batting first and our pitcher, Riley. Batting second and playing right field, Joe B. Batting third and catching is Juice. The fourth batter playing second base is Gravy. Fifth, and playing first base is Woody." Johnny hesitated because he was ahead of the players as they walked up and got in order. He wanted to let the families have a chance to cheer for their players. "The sixth batter is me, Johnny, who plays shortstop. Batting seventh and in center field is Chewey. At third base and batting eighth is Caldwell. Finally playing left field is Otis. Ready to come off the bench we have: Ray, Gimp, Wayne, Mat OB, Roy, and Guido. And the third base coach is Ricky T. Here they are everyone, this seasons Sully's Irish Pub lineup."

Everyone ate more BBQ and then it was time to head to the field for the first game against Tiny's Auto Supply and Towing.

Johnny arrived a few minutes after Ricky and joined him beside the dugout. "I guess it's game time. We are the home team, so I have a minute to get situated before we bat in the bottom of the first inning," Ricky said, adjusting his new hat and jersey. "Who is the umpire today?"

"Pete. He has been umpiring this league for years. He and Chad alternate between umping behind the plate and the bases," Johnny said.

There was not much action in the first couple of innings. Tiny's team was good but couldn't get many base runners off of Riley.

In the bottom of the third inning, Woody led off with a single. When Johnny moved him over to second base with another single, Sully's finally had a man in scoring position and Johnny decided to have Ray pinch run for Woody. The next batter was Chewey, who quickly was down two strikes after taking the first two pitches. On the third pitch, he swung and popped it up to the second baseman. One out in the inning. Next came Caldwell who hit a line drive to center field that dropped for a base hit. Ray took off from second base. Ricky checked the outfielder and then waved Ray home. He rounded third and dug in for home plate. It was going to be a close play at the plate. Ray slid into home plate.

"Out!" yelled the umpire.

"Come on, Pete. He was safe. Open your eyes!" Ricky yelled.

"You worry about third base, and I'll take care of calling the game. Okay, coach?" Pete responded.

"Ok, okay Pete. I'm just asking that you start calling the game with your eyes open." Ricky said.

The game was tied 0-0 at the bottom of the sixth. With one inning left, Sully's was up to bat and time was running out. Otis got a single. Riley grounded out. When Joe B came up to bat, the pitcher threw a flat pitch right down the middle of the plate. Joe B got a good swing on it and sent it over the right field fence. Sully's Pub took a 2-0 lead. In the top of the seventh inning, Sully's held on and won the game 2-1. The team had won their first game of the season, which always feels good.

After the game they went to the pub to celebrate. Ricky walked up to the bar and Riley saw him coming. "I'll have a Miller High Life," Ricky said.

Without a word, Riley reached into the cooler and handed him a Sam Boston. She gave him a smirk and moved on to the next customer.

"Why did you send Ray home in the third inning?" Johnny asked as he walked over. "We would have had bases loaded with one out."

"I watched him in practice. I thought he had the speed to make it," Ricky said, taking a sip of his beer.

"Well, you're the third base coach so it's your call," Johnny said.

"I got some background on Tommy and Gina. I'm thinking through my next step but will let you know when I come up with anything," Ricky said.

Chapter 4

Wednesday morning, Ricky stood in front of a medical building across from the hospital. After looking at the directory for a few seconds he found the name he was looking for: Dr. B. F. Pearce Room 202. Ricky walked through the double glass doors, went past the elevators, and took the stairs to the second floor.

He paused outside the door to gather himself, then removed his Red Sox hat and walked in. The receptionist, Margaret according to her name plate, greeted him as he entered.

"I have a 10:00 appointment with Dr. Pearce," Ricky said.

"Good morning, Mr. Temple. Dr. Pearce is expecting you. He will be ready to see you in a few minutes. Have a seat and I'll let him know you're here. We have a few forms for you to fill out as well," Margaret said. She handed him the standard doctor's office clipboard.

Ricky sat down and tried to get comfortable while filling out his forms. He had just finished when Margaret told him he could go in.

Ricky walked through the door and looked around. To his surprise there was no place to lie down. *I guess I watch too much TV,* he thought.

"Good morning, Dr. Pearce, I'm Ricky Temple," he said trying to appear at ease.

"Come on in Ricky. Just call me Ben, have a seat, and get comfortable. We have an hour or so to talk," Ben said. "I believe your wife made the appointment for you and said something about sleep problems because of some dreams you've been having. How long have you been having these dreams?"

"You know Ben, I'm on this softball team and there is this coach on another team that is giving us a hard time. I'm trying to figure it out. Sorry, I should have mentioned that I'm a private investigator," Ricky said to a confused-looking Ben. "I thought this was going to be a simple case but there seems to be much more to it. To better understand him, I'm looking into this guy's business to figure out why he is worked up all the time. His money doesn't make sense right now. You know what I mean? I keep trying to process it in my head, but it isn't connecting," Ricky said.

"Did I misunderstand? I thought you were having a dream or anxiety issue we need to talk about." Ben said.

"I think you're doing great, Ben. What gets me is there doesn't seem to be a money trail because if there was one my wife would have found it. So, how did this guy go from bankruptcy to opening a new business within months? Then he added two more stores," Ricky said, staring at the wall. "I think I know what I need to do next. Thanks Ben, this has been incredibly helpful. I'll talk to Margaret and set up my next appointment." Ricky stood to leave.

"Ricky, you've only been here 20 minutes, and I don't think we talked about your issue. All you talked about is your work," Ben said. He shrugged and watched his new patient leave his office.

Ricky stopped on his way out to make another appointment with Margaret.

"Same time next week if you have it. He is great, really helped me out," Ricky said. Once his next appointment was booked, he walked out of the office, back down the stairs, and out the two glass doors he had entered a short time ago. When he got back to his car, he called Susan.

"Hey, I know what we need to do next for the Tommy Bonetti case. We will need the Caddy," Ricky said.

"The Caddy? You haven't brought that out in a while. Wait, it's only 10:30, your session was for an hour. What happened?" she asked.

"We made a lot of progress. I like this Ben guy."

"Would Dr. Pearce agree that you made a lot of progress?" Susan asked.

"I guess so. He didn't say much. He just sat there with a weird look on his face," Ricky said. "I'll need you to give me a ride later to get the Caddy out of storage. I think softball practice will be cancelled today because it's supposed to rain. So, we have all afternoon."

Tommy told Neil and Jason to keep everybody away from his office and not to bother them. He and Gina had work to do. He locked the door, moved the rug, and opened the door that covered the door to his hiding place. Tommy went down the stairs and handed the suitcases to Gina. When all the suitcases were in the office, Tommy came back up, closed the door, and sat back down at his desk. The last thing he had to do was reach under his desk and pull the lever that released a compartment. He reached in, found their ledger, and handed it to Gina.

Gina opened the ledger as Tommy opened the first case. As usual, on top of the money was a piece of paper with the amount. They counted the money themselves to make sure the piece of paper was correct and that nobody 'borrowed' any money between Georgia and North Carolina. There were no discrepancies.

"Okay, so we have $50,000 in that case. We need to start depositing it into bank accounts. Then write the checks to our "tire distributors" in Atlanta and Newark. Next, we need to use our cut to pay our bills for the three Tommy's Tire Emporium locations. I don't want to ever run the risk of late payments or anything else that will bring attention to us," Tommy said.

"We also need to pay the expenses for our Atlanta friend's house down at High Rock Lake," Gina reminded him. "I think our next money shipment is the first of the month, by the way."

"I checked last week. We have $20,000 hidden downstairs as our runaway fund if things go bad. I think we will add another $5,000 to that and keep adding each month now that the shipments are more regular. We will need to refill the cases with the money from the drug sales and have Neil and Jason take them to the Charlotte and Athens stores. We do enough here and need to be careful to not bring attention to us," Tommy said.

"I took the call from Atlanta last night since you were busy. We discussed the latest information. They haven't heard anything about any Federal investigations into any of our efforts. They said they are going to increase the amount of money we need to move, and we should start thinking about opening another location. They like having distribution sites close to college campuses and want us to explore more of that. They also want me to calm things down with Johnny Sullivan, they don't want us bringing unneeded attention to us or them. Atlanta is going to have us start dropping some money at some of those hacker houses they set up," Tommy said. They started putting the drug money into the suitcases.

"That increase in cash makes me nervous, but I agree about calming things down," Gina said. "We have been able to avoid attention because we have been dealing with small amounts. The last thing we need is to get the Secret Service interested in us. Same goes for the drugs and the DEA," Gina said.

"I agree but if you think about it, we have the drugs, the money laundering, and we're being financed by an organized crime syndicate. That brings in multiple federal agencies like the DEA,

Secret Service, FBI, and they would all consult with local police. We aren't hearing about anything. Come on, with all that's involved, do you really think the Government would be able to keep it a secret?" Tommy asked.

When they were done, Tommy locked the door to the hiding space, moved his chair back behind his desk, and unlocked his office door. He felt they had a good morning. It only took an hour to deal with that work.

Tommy called Neil and Jason into his office.

"You two will need to make a run to Charlotte and Athens sometime in the next week or so. This time we are adding a stop in Greenville, South Carolina, too. No stopping this time. No strip clubs, no bars, no sampling of any of the product. The only difference is this time you will come back here to High Point instead of going to New Jersey. You understand?" Tommy said.

"Sure boss, we would never do anything like that," Jason said.

"Of course you wouldn't," Tommy replied.

Ricky and Susan sat on the back patio of their condo before she took him to Jamestown, North Carolina to get the Caddy. It was getting dark out and it looked like it would storm at any time.

"I think it's time to visit Tommy's Tire Emporium," Ricky said.

"You need to be careful, especially if he knows who you are," Susan warned.

"I know, but I want to see what kind of business he is doing. I've never been inside his store, and I want to see what's going on. Try to get a feel for how they have so much money. Since we have lived here, until Johnny said something about giving them a bad review, I've never heard of anyone going there for tires," Ricky said. He looked up at the sky as he heard a clap of thunder. "It's really looking like a good little storm is coming. Maybe we should get going," Ricky said.

"I'm ready whenever you are."

Ricky and Susan went to the garage and got in the silver Ford Escape that Ricky uses for work. Susan knew they would be driving the Escape and the Caddy until this was over. Ricky took the cover off the Escape, put it on the BMW, and then they both got in. He turned on the 80's satellite channel and started to sing along to the Kenny Rogers and Dolly Parton classic, 'Islands in the Stream,' off-key as usual. He looked over at Susan as she started her usual seat dancing.

As Ricky and Susan pulled out of their subdivision it started to rain. It wasn't coming down hard at first, but it picked up as they went. They drove to the highway and the rain stayed with them when they exited near Jamestown. It wasn't much further to the storage area. As they pulled in, the rain slowed to a drizzle, or as they say in the South, it was spittin'.

Ricky got out and walked around the corner to where he stored the Caddy, just out of sight of where Susan parked. He stood there for several seconds admiring his beautiful piece of machinery.

Susan heard him coming before she saw him. When she heard Aerosmith's 'Sweet Emotion' cranked, she knew he had the windows down and it would only be a matter of time before he pulled out.

As if on cue, Susan saw the front end of their 1996 turquoise Cadillac slowly coming toward her. She wanted to laugh, but she loved that car as much as Ricky did. As he pulled up beside her, she said, "Do you really need to wear those sunglasses? It's raining."

"It's part of the image," Ricky said.

"Why don't you get another tape? Doesn't it get old only listening to that one song when you're driving around?" she asked.

"First of all, it's a cassingle, so no way I'm changing it. Besides, this one is stuck in there. How about I meet you at home after I go to check out Tommy's? We can take her for a ride down to Sully's," Ricky said.

"I'll be waiting for you," she said.

Ricky left the storage facility and drove 20 minutes to Tommy's Tire Emporium. A block away from the store, he turned the music down and parked down the street. He wanted to watch the store for a few minutes before venturing in.

This really seems odd. There are no cars in the parking lot, no cars near the service bays either. The only sign of life is the neon "Open" sign lit up, and the van parked on the corner, Ricky thought.

After 15 minutes, Ricky pulled the Caddy into the parking lot and went inside. He noticed two salesmen standing near a cash register, what appeared to be an office door on the back right side, and another door on the back left that led to the work bays. He memorized the layout so he could draw a sketch of it later. The two salesmen approached.

"Can we help you, Mister...?" Neil asked.

"How ya doing, I'm Tom Hagen. I want to talk to someone about getting some white walls for the Caddy out there. She's a beauty, isn't she?" Ricky said, pointing toward his parked car.

"Nice to meet you, Mr. Hagen. I'm Neil and this is Jason. Yes, that's a nice-looking automobile you have there. We should be able to help you out," Neil said.

"Just call me Tom. Yeah, I've been wanting to put some white walls on her for some time, and I woke up this morning and told the Missus that today is the day. Are you boys running any specials?" Ricky asked.

"I'm sure we can work something out. I don't think we have any in stock but will be happy to order some for you," Jason said.

"Don't have any in stock? I thought this was supposed to be a big-time tire store! White walls are the classiest tires you can buy. They should always be in stock. How long will it take if you order them and what will it cost me?" Ricky asked.

Jason walked over to the computer and started typing. "And you want four, right Tom?" he asked.

"Of course I want four. Two doesn't do me any good," Ricky replied. It was clear to Ricky that these two weren't seasoned tire salesmen. He noticed the office door start to open and then close quietly. He swore he saw someone looking through the blinds.

"And what size do you want?" Neil asked. He had moved over to the computer to try to help Jason.

"You're the salesman, you tell me what works best. I'm not here to tell you your business," Ricky said.

"Sorry Tom, the computer seems to be down right now, so we can't quote you a price. Would you be willing to come back later?" Jason asked, trying to end the sale and get Ricky out of the store.

"Well, I guess I can do that. I'll come back tomorrow," Ricky said.

"Sounds good, we will see you then."

Neil and Jason watched as Ricky drove off. As soon as he was out of the parking lot, the office door opened.

"What was that all about?" Tommy asked. Gina stood beside him, also waiting for an answer.

"Oh, that was some guy named Tom Hagen. He wants to buy some white wall tires for his car," Neil said.

"That was Tom Hagen?" Tommy asked.

"Yeah, that's what he said, Tom Hagen," Jason said.

"You think that was Tom Hagen. You idiots! Tom Hagen is a character from the Godfather movies. That was Ricky Temple, a local PI!" Tommy yelled. "One of you needs to keep an eye on him and figure out why he was in here using a fake name."

When Ricky left Tommy's Tires, he drove a short distance to be out of sight of the store and pulled into a parking lot to think. *That was weird. Neither of them seemed to know anything about tires. There are very few tires on display, and no cars in the service bays either. What is going on? Was it just a slow day? Were those two just new salesmen? Who was watching through the blinds in the office? It had to be either Tommy or Gina.*

He drove home and picked up Susan to go back downtown for drinks at Sully's. Ricky told Susan the story about his experience at the tire store as they drove to the pub. As usual, he parked across the street.

They walked in and saw Riley was behind the bar. She got a glass of Chablis for Susan and set it on the bar.

"Hey Riley, how's it going?" Ricky asked. "I think I'll have a Miller High Life."

"Ricky, you know we don't serve it here. You'll have a Sam Boston and like it," Riley said.

Business was slow, so the three friends talked for a while.

"Johnny is going to text everyone later, but we are going to practice tomorrow. He wants to get one more in before the big game against Tommy's. I think he said 5:00 p.m. at Hedgecock Park," Riley said.

"Sounds good. I'll be there. Hopefully the rain clears out," Ricky said. "You know, we are looking good so far. With a record of 2-0 and tied for first place with Tommy's Tires, that game is huge."

"I know. Tucker's Paint isn't too far behind, either. We beat them and they lost to Tommy's. I feel bad for Tiny's, they are 0-2," Riley said.

"I know, but we need to worry about us. I'll see you at practice tomorrow," Ricky said. He and Susan finished their drinks and left.

"Task Force Base, this is Surveillance 1, over."

"Go ahead Surveillance 1, this is Base."

"We had new activity at the target business. A turquoise Cadillac arrived and stayed at the target business for about 10 minutes. Prior to entering the store, the driver of the Cadillac, an adult male in his early to mid-50's with grey hair, parked at the end of the street. He appeared to be watching the store prior to going in. I have a license plate when you are ready to copy."

"Go ahead Surveillance 1, send it."

Chapter 5

FBI Special Agent Chester Monroe pulled into the High Point Post Office parking lot, got out, and walked up the loading ramp past the workers loading the mail trucks for the day's deliveries. He entered the building and went down one flight to the basement where the newly formed Federal Task Force was setting up.

Special Agent Monroe's desk was in the middle of the room where the senior special agents from the other agencies were located: the DEA, Secret Service, ATF, High Point Police Department, Guilford County Sheriff Office, and the North Carolina State Highway Patrol all had desks in the middle of the room and were surrounded by the junior agents. He stood there looking around, content that more desks were filling up by the day.

"Anything new this morning?" Special Agent Monroe asked his partner.

"We had something at the target business," Special Agent Mitch Johnston said. "Yesterday afternoon a turquoise Cadillac registered to Ricky Temple of High Point was hanging around the store. He went in and stayed about 10 minutes before leaving. I ran the name by the local police who said he is a local PI. We ran him on the federal side overnight, the info just came in. He retired from the military and worked in Special Operations with multiple deployments. Not too surprising, there isn't much on the operations he worked on."

"Interesting. Wonder why he's poking around? Last thing we need is a local PI cowboy getting in our way," Special Agent Monroe said. "If he shows up again, put a guy on him. Is the cyber investigation team set up yet?"

"They should be set up today. Once they get going, the intelligence team will give info to the cyber forensic guy and the cyber hunters who work to identify threats," Special Agent Johnston said.

Special Agent Monroe was happy to hear the surveillance van was already in place. He knew they would place listening devices inside the business as soon as the warrants came down from the Assistant U.S. Attorney. He was hoping that would happen in the next 48 hours.

Ricky grabbed a cup of coffee from the kitchen and went into the office to see what Susan was working on. She had printed a map of High Point and marked key locations and placed picture of Tommy Bonetti at the location of the Tire Emporium. She then placed marks at Sully's Pub, and the softball fields the league uses.

"It's not perfect, but it's a start," Susan said as Ricky looked at her work. "Are you going to move the Caddy? You know the HOA won't like it parked out front."

"Screw the HOA. I had Father Tim read the bylaws when we worked with him in Asheville. He said their document is weak and we could press them in court if we ever needed to," Ricky said.

It would be great to see Father Tim, Susan thought. Father Tim is an ordained priest who is also a lawyer. Both of his professions came into play during their last case.

I wonder if Ricky will call RJ again, Susan thought. RJ Floyd and Ricky were old Army buddies. They went through a lot together when they were still active duty and Ricky calls him for help sometimes.

"I know I told you on the way home last night, but it's really bugging me. Something just wasn't right at Tommy's. I know there are plenty of reasons why there was nobody there, but my gut feeling is that something isn't right," Ricky said.

"What are you thinking?" Susan asked.

"I think I'm going to take another look. I'm not going inside this time. If someone really was watching from the office, they would have recognized me. Although his two salesmen were clueless," Ricky said.

"Be careful. If he did see you, he might be waiting for you," Susan said.

"I will," Ricky said. "Remember we have practice tonight. Hopefully it will be uneventful." Ricky grabbed his Red Sox hat and the keys to the Caddy.

When Ricky got to the Caddy, there was a note on the windshield. It was a warning from the HOA about parking on the street. He crumpled it up, threw it on the ground, got in, and drove off.

Fifteen minutes later, Ricky drove past Tommy's and parked across the street. He walked into the laundromat and sat down to watch the front door of Tommy's Tire Emporium.

"Task Force Base, this is Surveillance 1, over."

"Go ahead Surveillance 1."

"Roger, the turquoise Cadillac is back. The driver went into the laundromat. Not sure what he is doing, we don't have a good view of the inside."

"Copy all. Was he carrying anything?"

"Negative."

"Surveillance 1 standby."

"Special Agent Monroe?" I have the radio watch right now. We just got a report from Surveillance 1."

"What's going on?" Special Agent Monroe asked.

"The turquoise Cadillac from yesterday is back at the target business. The driver parked, got out, and went into a laundromat. We were briefed at shift change to notify you if it showed up again."

"Thanks, I do want to know when that car shows up. We are getting a picture of the driver ready for everyone. This guy is smart and may show up in different cars. Tell Surveillance 1 we are going to roll a car to follow and intercept him," Special Agent Monroe said.

Pretty much the same as yesterday, Ricky thought. He sat just inside the door of the laundromat with a good view of the parking lot and front door of Tommy's Tires. *No cars in the parking lot, nobody going in or out of the front door. No cars near the service bays and the same van parked in the grocery store parking lot instead of on the edge of the street. Wait. How did I miss that? It's the same van as yesterday in a different spot,* Ricky thought. He took out a notepad and wrote down the description. Light brown conversion van, two small antennas on top.

"Damn it, how did I miss that yesterday?" Ricky yelled, surprising the other laundromat customers.

"I need to get the license plate number over to Susan," Ricky said out loud as he got up to leave. He didn't notice the strange looks he was getting from the other customers.

The FBI team assigned to follow and intercept Ricky Temple pulled into the parking lot just as their subject was getting into his car. The two agents radioed to the Task Force Base they were on scene and had had eyes on the vehicle.

"Okay, he's leaving. Let's go," the agent in the passenger seat said.

Ricky pulled out of his parking space toward the street. He stopped to wait for a gap in the traffic before pulling out. He pulled out and turned right at the stop light. He decided to drop by Sully's Pub to have a beer and think.

After he turned, he noticed a blue Buick behind him. *Where did he come from? That looks like a cop car all day long,* Ricky thought. At the next intersection, he got into the right lane. The Buick stayed behind him.

Two guys are in the car, and he's still behind me. Am I being followed? Let's make another turn to see if I'm imagining things, Ricky thought. He kept going for several blocks before turning right again. *This will bring us right back to where we just started. Four rights are a circle,* Ricky thought. He pulled up to the stop sign where he started. Tommy's Tires was on his right, and the brown van was still across the street. He turned right again, completing the circle. The blue Buick came with him.

"What's going on? All he did was make a big circle. Do you think he made us?" the driver said.

"Either he made us, or this was part of whatever he is up to. To be safe, let's call in for another team to take over."

Before they had the chance to ask for help, Ricky's car sped up and took off.

Ricky looked in the rearview mirror as he sped away. The Buick accelerated to catch up. Ricky turned up his 'Sweet Emotion' cassingle as loud as it would go. His blood was flowing. He wasn't sure if it was the police or some of Tommy's guys behind him. Either way, he wanted them off his tail, especially since he didn't know why they were following him.

Ricky was flying now. Once the Caddy got up to speed, it was unstoppable. He stayed on North Centennial Street as he went over the railroad tracks. The Cadillac fishtailed when he took a quick turn, but Ricky got control back. He had forgotten the difference between the handling of a Cadillac and a BMW. The Buick wasn't too far behind.

Ricky got into the right lane, but the light was red. The Buick got in the lane next to him. Just as the Buick got beside him, he saw the passenger reach for something. Ricky looked in his rearview mirror and liked what he saw. He threw the Cadillac in reverse and stomped on the gas pedal. The driver and passenger of the Buick had 'oh shit' looks on their faces. Another car pulled up behind the Buick. As Ricky passed that car, he took his foot off the gas, whipped the steering wheel to the left to make a 180-degree turn, put the Caddy into drive, and took off. The Buick was blocked in.

Ricky stayed on East Commerce Avenue until he got several blocks away. He slowed down but the tires still squealed as he made a few turns to ensure the Buick couldn't find him. He pulled into a large parking lot, went all the way to the back near the Guilford County Register of Deeds, and parked under a tree. He had no idea he was only a block away from the Task Force Operations Center.

"Task Force base, this is the Surveillance 2, over."

"Go ahead surveillance 2."

"We lost him. Returning to base."

"Copy."

The radio watch stander walked over to Special Agent Monroe. "Sir, the team sent to follow the Cadillac lost him. They aren't sure where he is now."

"It's a turquoise Cadillac! How did they lose it?" he yelled.

"I'm not sure, but the agents are returning here now," the watch stander said. He turned to go back to his position.

Special Agent Monroe turned to his partner. "Get me Temple's address. Let's go over there and see what he has to say."

Once Ricky caught his breath, he called Susan. "Hey, I had an interesting turn of events," he said.

"That doesn't sound good. What happened?" she asked.

"I was sitting in the laundromat watching the store when it hit me. The last two days, the same brown conversion van has been parked near Tommy's Tire Emporium. In different spots but always there. I drove by to get the license plate. When I left, I was followed by the FBI. I was able to lose them. The Caddy did good. I forgot how hard it is to handle her when she's going fast, though," Ricky said, still coming down from the adrenaline.

"How do you know it was the FBI?" Susan asked.

"I saw the two guys in the car when I sped away. They were wearing dark suits and red ties with sunglasses, driving a basic blue Buick. The classic FBI uniform. Can you listen to your police scanner? Let me know if you hear anything about me or the Caddy," he said.

"If it was the FBI, I doubt we would hear anything on the police scanner," she said.

"True, but if there is another agency involved you might. I'm heading for Sully's to get out of sight until we know something. I'll call when I get there. Oh yeah, I almost forgot, here is the license plate for the van. See what you can find out," Ricky said. He read her the license plate number and hung up.

Ricky went back the way he had come on South Centennial Street, working his way to the backside of Sully's Irish Pub. He pulled into the small parking lot behind Sully's, got out, and locked the doors.

Ricky walked down the hallway past Johnny's office and the bathrooms. He knocked on the office door, but there was no answer. He wasn't surprised since he had just parked in Johnny's empty space. Ricky continued down the short hall to the bar and saw Riley.

"Where's Johnny?" he asked.

"Not here yet. Something wrong?" Riley asked.

"No. I just need to talk to him. I'll give him a call. Can I get a Miller High Life?" Ricky said.

Riley reached into the beer cooler and handed him a Sam Boston. Ricky took it and walked over to a table in the corner. He needed to think. Before he could process his most recent adventure, he heard someone yell from the back of the bar.

"WHO THE HELL IS PARKED IN MY SPOT?"

Ricky realized it was Johnny and jumped up to meet him by his office.

"I just need to park there until after practice, then I'm heading home. I had a busy morning and need to lay low for a bit," Ricky said.

"Lay low? What's going on?"

"I'm trying to put the pieces of the puzzle together and need a place where I can think about your case," Ricky said.

After defusing Johnny, Ricky went back to his table and called Susan.

"Hey, have you heard anything on the scanner?" he asked.

"No. It's quiet. The usual stuff. Mainly traffic stops," Susan told him.

"What about the license plate? Anything on that yet?" he asked.

"I haven't gotten to it yet. I was getting a snack first," Susan said. "Hold on a minute, someone is at the door."

Susan looked out the window to see who it was. "Ricky, I might have a problem. Two guys in suits and sunglasses are at the front door. A blue Buick is in the driveway."

"Crap. Let's hang up and you see what they want. Be non-committal about everything," he warned.

Susan closed the blinds, walked out, and shut the office door. She took a couple of deep breaths, put on a big smile, and opened the front door.

"Mrs. Temple? I'm Special Agent Monroe and this is Special Agent Johnston of the FBI." They held their credentials open for her to see. "Is your husband home? We need to talk to him."

"No. Ricky isn't here. I'm not sure when he will be back. Is there something I can help you with?" Susan asked.

"Maybe. May we come in and talk?" Special Agent Johnston asked.

"Sure. Come on in. Would you like some sweet tea? I just made a new pitcher," she asked.

"No thank you. We are working on a case and would like to talk to Ricky about some things he has been doing over the last few days," Special Agent Johnston said.

Susan noticed the other agent was looking around the living room and not really paying attention. "What kind of things?" she asked. Susan wanted to get as much information from them as they were trying to get from her.

"He has been seen hanging around some businesses downtown and we just wanted to know what the local PI was working on," he said.

"You mean private investigator," Susan said. It was the first time she got to correct someone, and she enjoyed it. "I'm not sure what he is working on, but I can ask him to get in touch with you. Do you have a card I can give him?" she asked signaling the end of her cooperation.

Susan had barely finished her sentence when two business cards were put in front of her.

"The sooner we hear from him, the better. We would hate to have to locate him ourselves," Special Agent Monroe said.

Susan took that as a threat and did not like it. After they left, she went back to the office to call Ricky.

"I think she was lying," said Special Agent Johnston. "She knows exactly what he is working on.

"I agree. I don't like it either, but let's sit on it for a day. If we don't hear from Temple by close of business tomorrow, we will find him and bring him in ourselves," Special Agent Monroe said.

Ricky was getting nervous. It had been twenty minutes since he had hung up with Susan. He walked over to the bar to get another beer.

"I'll take a Miller High Life and a Powers Gold Label Irish Whiskey," Ricky said to Riley.

"Are you sure? Don't forget we have practice in a little while," she said.

"I'm the third base coach. How much practicing am I going to do?" he said.

"Good point. Are you okay?" Riley asked. She got a Sam Boston out of the cooler and then poured him a whiskey.

"Yeah, I'm good," Ricky said as his phone rang.

"What happened?" Ricky asked, not giving Susan a chance to say hello.

"You were right. It's the FBI. A Special Agent Monroe, who seemed to be in charge, and Special Agent Johnston. They want to talk to you about what you are working on. They said you have been hanging around some businesses the last couple of days and want to know why," Susan said.

"What am I in the middle of? I was just trying to learn more about this softball coach and get him off Johnny's back, and now the FBI is involved," Ricky said partially to Susan and partially to no one. "Did they say anything else?"

"Just that they want you to get in touch with them as soon as you can. They said it would be best for you to contact them, so they don't have to locate you themselves," she said. "It pissed me off, but I had already ended the discussion. I had even offered them some of the sweet tea I had just made."

"That sounds like a threat," Ricky said, drinking down his whiskey. "I talked to Johnny. I'm leaving the Caddy here. I'll pick it up after practice. He will give me a ride back here for beers with the team and then I'll be home."

"You're still going to practice? Just come home," Susan said.

"I want to act as if nothing is wrong. They won't be back at the house until tomorrow night or the next day at the earliest. They'll give me a chance to come to them. If they wanted me now, you would be hearing it on the scanners because they would get the local police's help. My guess is they aren't sure where I fit. Hell, I don't even know where I fit in," Ricky said.

"Okay, but be careful," Susan said.

As Ricky hung up, Johnny came out of his office to get him to head over to practice. They walked out, got into Johnny's car, and headed for the field.

At practice, Ricky hit ground balls to the infield while Johnny hit fly balls to the outfield. When the last batter had taken a few swings, Johnny called everyone together.

"Big game tomorrow night. Tommy's Tires, so it's a battle for first place. The game is at 6:00 p.m., so everyone, try to get here at 5:30 to warm up. That's all I got. Woody, you and Otis gather everything up. We'll meet you at the pub, good practice everyone."

It was 8:00 p.m. when Ricky walked through the door of the condo. Susan was waiting for him, sitting on the couch watching a movie while eating some cheese and crackers.

"Any issues?" she asked.

"No. It was a smooth night. Practice was short since we have a big game tomorrow night. Are you coming?" he said.

"I wouldn't miss seeing whatever is going to happen between Sully's and Tommy's. What about the FBI?" she asked.

"I've been thinking about that. The smart thing would be for me to meet with them to see what they say. Who knows, maybe I can get some info out of them and give up very little in return. I'll call them in the morning. See where it goes from there," Ricky said. He took a piece of cheese from Susan's plate.

Chapter 6

Ricky and Susan sat outside having coffee. It was a warm and humid morning. They liked to sit outside in the mornings as long as they could, before the full heat of summer set in.

"What else did the FBI guy say?" Ricky asked, breaking the silence.

"Just what I told you. They want to talk to you about whatever you're working on. What are you going to do?" she asked.

"I guess I'll call him. Maybe it will shed some light on what I'm in the middle of. Where are the business cards they gave you?" he asked.

"Right here. I felt like Special Agent Monroe was in charge. I would call him first."

"Okay, let's see what he has to say," Ricky said. He picked up his phone and put in the number.

"Is this Chet?" Ricky asked.

"This is Special Agent Chester Monroe. Who's calling?"

"Chet, this is Ricky Temple. I believe you came to my house and questioned my wife yesterday. What do you want?" Ricky asked.

"I assume your wife told you that I'm a Special Agent with the FBI. We want to talk to you about the case you're working on. What time today can we meet?" he asked.

"I'll have to look at my calendar and call you back," Ricky said. *Click.*

"That was a little aggressive, don't you think?" Susan said.

"No, not really. Did I say anything that wasn't true?" he asked.

"Well, no," she replied.

"Chet is fishing. Just like me, he has no idea where I fit into whatever is going on. He wants to meet in person to try to intimidate me. He'll show up with at least one other agent. They'll flash their badges around and talk like they know more than they do," Ricky said. "I'll call him back in an hour or so. I think I'll suggest a meeting place that's on the way to the game tonight."

"Okay, but keep in mind it is the FBI, so I wouldn't push too hard," Susan advised.

It was 11:00 a.m. when they went back inside to clean up after breakfast. Ricky went into the office and sat down in Susan's chair to think through what he knew. After a few minutes, it was time to call Chet back.

"I was wondering if you would call back," Special Agent Monroe answered.

"I'll be at the Coffee Bar at 3:00 p.m. Do you know where that is?" Ricky asked.

"No, but I'll find it. We will be there," Special Agent Monroe said. *Click.*

Ricky wrote a note to put on the board. *FBI isn't familiar with the area. They are from out of town.* He posted it on the board as Susan walked in.

"How did it go?" she asked.

"I learned these FBI agents aren't local. This might be bigger than we think," Ricky said.

Ricky knew it was going to be a long day, so he took a nap before his meeting with the Feds and the big game. At 2:30 p.m., Ricky got ready to leave for his meeting with the FBI. He wanted to be the first one there so he could see if they put anyone in place ahead of time. He gathered everything he needed for the game, put on his Red Sox hat, and started out the door.

"Be careful. I'll see you at the game and I'll get there a few minutes early so we can talk," Susan said.

Ricky gave her a kiss and walked to the Caddy. As he got to his car, he took the note from the HOA off his windshield and threw it on the ground. He got in, cranked up 'Sweet Emotion' and drove off.

Fifteen minutes later, he pulled into the Coffee Bar parking lot, adjusted his Red Sox hat, and made sure his uniform was ready for the game before going inside. The FBI was already there. Ricky walked in and saw the two men sitting in the back corner wearing their standard dark suits, dress shoes, and red ties. He looked around to see if he could spot any other agents in normal clothes. Satisfied, it was just the two in the corner, he ordered a coffee and walked to the back of the café.

"You must be Chet," Ricky said as he approached the table.

The two agents stood and pulled out their credentials. "Mr. Temple, I'm Special Agent Chester Monroe and this is Special Agent Mitch Johnston. Have a seat."

"Why is the FBI in town?" Ricky said, wanting to take control of the conversation.

"Why don't you think we're assigned to High Point permanently?" Special Agent Johnston asked.

"Because Chet didn't know where this place was. It's a popular coffee shop on North Main Street, right in the middle of town, to start with," Ricky said.

The two agents looked at each other. Maybe they underestimated this guy.

"We are just wondering what the local PI is working on?" Special Agent Monroe asked.

"First of all, Chet, I'm a private investigator and I'm not working on anything. I don't understand why you think I am. What's the FBI's interest, anyway?" Ricky replied.

"Yes, your wife told us yesterday that it's private investigator. You've been going by Tommy's Tire Emporium a lot lately," he said.

"My Cadillac needs some tires. I want to get some white walls. Was I supposed to check with the FBI before I buy tires?" Ricky asked. He smiled to himself that Susan had corrected the FBI.

"If you were only looking to buy tires, why did you speed away from the store the other day?' the agent asked.

"I don't like being followed and got concerned with the FBI surveillance," Ricky shot back.

"What FBI surveillance?" Special Agent Monroe asked.

"You see Chet, I'm not as dumb as you want me to be. The brown conversion van with multiple antennas on top that has been sitting in front of the tire store for the last few days, looks a lot like a surveillance vehicle to me. The blue Buick, much like the one parked outside right now, followed me. The two agents who were following me probably need an offensive driving refresher course. I haven't heard my Miranda rights, so that means I'm not under arrest for buying tires. I have a big softball game tonight, so I have to go," Ricky said. He stood up and walked out.

Riley Simms was sitting under a tree behind the dugout singing along to Kenny Chesney when Ricky pulled into Allen Jay Park. He was surprised to find almost all the parking spaces were taken. He got out of the Caddy, put on his jersey, and switched his Red Sox hat for his Sully's hat. He was ready.

A few minutes after he joined the team they started laughing and cheering. Ricky turned to see Susan walking toward him wearing a t-shirt that said 'The 3B Base Coach Is Hot.' Ricky walked over, gave her a hug, and whispered in her ear, "Let's talk."

They walked to a tree that was away from everybody.

"What happened at the coffee shop?" Susan asked when they were alone.

"It was quick. They wanted to know why I've been hanging around Tommy's so much lately and why I sped away from the tire store," he said.

"I'm afraid to ask, but what did you tell them?"

"I told them I needed some white walls, and I don't like being followed by FBI surveillance. They asked, "What FBI surveillance?' That pissed me off, so I dropped it all on them. The brown conversion van and the blue Buick. I even pointed to the Buick in the parking lot. They made me mad, so I left. I'm sure we will hear from them again," Ricky said. "And good job on correcting them on the PI thing. It made me laugh."

Susan smiled. "I'm sure we will be hearing from them again. I wonder what Tommy Bonetti is into?" she asked.

"I don't know, but since we are in the middle of it now, we need to figure it out," Ricky said. He turned to see Tommy and Gina yelling at Sully's team as they walked into their dugout.

"Looks like the game is about to start. We are the home team today, so I'd better get to the dugout. Great shirt by the way," Ricky said.

The top of the first inning was uneventful. Gina grounded out to first base to end the inning. Ricky jogged out to his place as the third base coach. He wasn't there long as it was quick bottom of the inning as well. Ricky didn't have much to do but stand there and pretend like he was giving the batters signals, but he gave it his all.

After the other employees left for the day, Neil and Jason lined up the suitcases of money Tommy had left for them outside his office. They double checked that they had them all before loading the car. The last thing they wanted was to mess it up. Tommy was still mad about that Temple guy the other day.

"Everything is loaded. I think we are ready to go," Jason said.

"Good. It looks like we will just go down I-85 like the last time," Neil said.

They pulled out of Tommy's Tire Emporium and drove toward the highway.

In the second inning the talk between the dugouts increased. Juice and Gravy decided before the game they weren't taking any crap from Tommy's team. By the third inning, Tommy's had a one run lead, and it was Sully's turn to hit.

Chewey was up to bat, and he looked toward Ricky. Ricky gave his usual signals. Gina's pitch came right toward Chewey's knees. It appeared to everyone it was thrown that way on purpose. The entire team in Sully's dugout stood up to yell at Gina.

Gina threw the next pitch. Chewey was ready and knocked it into center field. Chewey is a fast guy and stretched the single into a double. Ricky gave him the stop sign. He would easily beat the tag but slid hard into Tommy's shortstop at second base. By the time Chewey stood up, the shortstop was yelling in his face. Chewey gave him a good shove. Chad, the umpire, broke it up and tried to restore order to the game.

Caldwell was up next. He jumped on the first pitch and hit a single to shallow left field. Ricky waved Chewey home. The game was tied.

"We need to calm this down," Johnny said to Ricky as the team took the field for the fourth inning.

"Yeah, the trash talk is getting worse as the game goes on," Ricky said.

Before the inning started, Johnny called everyone to the pitcher's mound. "I know we don't like these guys, but let's remember this is supposed to be fun. Riley is pitching a great game and is getting a lot of ground balls, keeping them off base. Keep it up. Let's have a good last three innings and get to the bar for beers," Johnny said.

"What are you stalling for, Johnny? Are you guys scared of something? Let's play!" Tommy yelled.

Neil and Jason made it to Concord, North Carolina without noticing they were being followed. Suddenly, two North Carolina

Highway Patrol cruisers sped onto the highway with their lights flashing.

"I wonder where they are going?" Neil said, looking at the flashing blue lights in the rearview mirror.

Jason turned around and saw the patrol cars closing in on them fast. "Stay in the right lane and make sure you are going the speed limit," Jason said.

"I am. We haven't been above the speed limit since we left. Maybe there's an accident up ahead of us," Neil said.

One of the patrol cars sped past them and changed lanes to get in front of them as the other patrol car took up a position behind them. The rear patrol car hit his siren, and the three cars pulled onto the shoulder.

Before the officer got to the driver's side window, Jason texted, *Pulled over.* A grey Buick with no markings stopped in front of the front patrol car. Two guys got out wearing dark suits and ties.

"This can't be good," Neil said. "Let Tommy know."

Sitting in the dugout for the bottom of the fifth inning, Tommy heard a notification on one of his phones. He picked it up and yelled, "Shit!" Gina walked over to see what happened.

"Oh no," she said. "They'd better follow procedure and destroy the phones as fast as they can. As well as forgetting our names."

"Tommy, you're up!" yelled his first baseman.

Tommy, wanting another line of cocaine, walked to home plate. He looked annoyed. Ricky noticed and walked to the edge of the dugout and called Susan over. He whispered, "Did you see that? Tommy got a text and now he's mad. Something happened."

"What do you think?" she asked.

"Not sure. Stay here for a little while longer and let's see if we notice anything else. If I wave at you, head home and get on your police scanner and see if you hear anything. It might give us some indication of what is going on," Ricky said.

"Sounds good," Susan replied.

As Susan got back to her seat with the other wives and girlfriends, Tommy got a hit to center field. He rounded first. On his way to second, he shoved Woody in the back. Johnny was in position to take the throw from Chewey and put the tag on Tommy. Chewey had seen Tommy shove Woody, so he threw the ball directly at Tommy and hit him in the back.

The fuse that was already lit, ignited. Both dugouts emptied onto the field. Everyone looked for someone wearing the other jersey to punch. Ricky was in the middle of it with the rest of his teammates. He went straight for Tommy while Gina tried to get to Riley. Pete and Chad, the umpires, pulled players apart as best they could. Someone would get knocked down but would jump right back up looking for someone to hit. Ricky took as many punches as he threw.

The brawl went on for 10 minutes before order was restored. When the umpires finally broke up the fight, Ricky looked at Susan in the stands and gave her a wave.

Neil and Jason stood on the side of I-85 South in handcuffs, watching the two men in suits and the state troopers open the suitcases that had been in the back of their rental car. There were hundreds of thousands of dollars in cash inside. They both knew the procedure and had memorized the phone number for an attorney who had no connection to Tommy or his Tire Emporium.

The cars traveling on I-85 South near Concord slowed down to watch as two handcuffed guys were escorted to an unmarked grey Buick. Traffic was backed up for a mile.

With order restored, the game remained tied at 1-1. Pete and Chad decided not to throw anyone out of the game. Both sides were bruised, cut up, and sore from the brawl. It was the bottom of the seventh inning, so it was up to Sully's Irish Pub to score a run or go to extra innings. Everyone involved wanted this ugly game to end, especially Tommy. He needed to get to one of his other burner phones, to find out what was going on. For now, he tried to keep his head in the game.

Otis stepped up to the plate. Ricky wasn't watching the game much anymore. His eyes were glued to Tommy, who looked worried. Ricky was still trying to figure out what was happening when he heard a loud cheer. He looked up in time to see the ball go over the fence. Otis hit a homerun. Game over, Sully's Irish Pub won and took first place in the league.

Father Tim Daniels walked into Circus Act Brewery in Asheville, North Carolina. Livingston the bartender asked, "Hey Father Tim, do you want your usual stout?"

"Thanks Livingston, that would be great. Is Clif around today" Father Tim replied.

"No, just me today. He and his wife went to visit her parents at the retirement community. Pays to be the owner," Livingston said.

Father Tim looked up at the TV and was happy to see the Milwaukee Brewers game was on. He was excited anyway because he was just a few days away from starting his vacation. He had arranged with the Diocese of Charlotte for a nice long two-week vacation.

He would first go to High Point to see his uncle and hopefully have dinner with Ricky and Susan. After that, he would head to Lake Hartwell in South Carolina for a family reunion.

"Livingston, how much do I owe you tonight?" Father Tim asked.

"No check for you, Sport, you know your money is no good here. And next time you talk to Ricky T., tell him I still have some of his Miller High Life here. Nobody will drink it," Livingston said.

"Thanks, Livingston. I'll tell him and make sure you tell Clif I said hello. I'll catch up with him at mass on Saturday," Father Tim said.

The back corner of Sully's Irish Pub was littered with empty beer bottles and ice packs. The team was still running on adrenaline an hour after the game and was enjoying Dropkick Murphys playing overhead. Ricky walked over to Riley.

"You pitched a great game tonight," he said.

"Thanks Ricky. I was surprised you threw a few nice punches out there," she said.

"I bet it feels good to be on this side of the bar for a change and let Samantha bartend tonight," Ricky said.

"It's a nice change for sure. That was a wild one. Gina was coming at me like she wanted to kill me," Riley said.

"Hang in there, you did good tonight," Ricky said. He walked over to Johnny.

"Johnny, I gotta head for home. Before I leave, you need to know there's something going on. During the game, I saw Tommy get a text or phone call that really bothered him. There's more but I'll spare you for now. Something is going on around here and I'm in the middle of it. How's your knee?" Ricky said.

"I thought something changed quick in him. He was being his usual pain in the ass the entire game, but I could tell something happened right before he came up to bat. Fill me in when you can. The knee is good, it might be sore tomorrow," Johnny said. He turned to the team and yelled, "No practice tomorrow! Drink up. Good win."

Twenty minutes later, Ricky parked the turquoise Cadillac and went inside, happy to be home after a long day.

"Nice win, third base coach," Susan said as he sat down. "I've been listening to the scanner since I got home but haven't heard anything. The 11:00 p.m. news will start in about an hour, so we should see if there is anything on that."

Ricky opened the beer she gave him and put an ice pack on his eye to try to help with the swelling. "Waiting for the news is a good idea. Something is going on, the look on his face said a lot."

"While we wait, I found that news report you were talking about the other day. You were right. About four years ago, some FBI sting money showed up here in High Point. The article said it was from an undercover operation they were running in Atlanta.

Different denominations showed up at a few businesses and bars around town. Before the FBI could get anywhere it suddenly stopped," Susan said.

"Interesting. We have the FBI here possibly watching Tommy's Tire Emporium and now we find this report from a few years ago. It could all be a coincidence, I guess," Ricky said.

Ricky and Susan had another drink and talked more about the game. At 11:00 Susan turned on the news. They didn't have to wait long. When the lead story was over, Susan turned the TV off and looked at Ricky. "What do you think?" she asked.

"That's a hell of a coincidence; two guys stopped on I-85 South by the highway patrol. Did you notice the footage from the news helicopter? In front of the patrol cars was what looked like a Buick and two guys in suits. I also saw three suitcases on the side of the road," Ricky said. "We need to keep an eye on that as well."

"Anything yet?" Special Agent Monroe asked the watch stander.

"Initial reports are starting to come in. We should have more in a few minutes," she responded.

"No media! Does everyone hear me? No anonymous sources, no nothing. We will formulate a statement and send it through the North Carolina Highway Patrol!" Special Agent Monroe yelled so everyone in the operation center could hear.

"Sir, we didn't get as much as we hoped," a junior member of the Task Force said. "Three suitcases full of money in different denominations. We are counting it now. Inside the car were two smashed phones. We are sending them to the digital forensics team now, but we aren't expecting much. The two suspects were driving a rental car, which we already knew, and they both had Georgia driver's licenses. Neither one is talking, and they immediately asked to call their lawyer. They were separated as usual, and one of them called a lawyer, who is flying up from Atlanta. He should be in the area in a few hours."

"Crap. Okay, I'm going home to get some sleep. Let's hope we get somewhere tomorrow," Special Agent Monroe said as he stood to put his jacket on. "And tell the agents that were on scene I want to see them in the morning."

"Special Agent Johnston, walk with me," Special Agent Monroe said as the watch stander walked back to the command post. "When the two were separated after the stop, did we get Neil out?"

"We did. We already started his debriefing," Special Agent Johnston said. "It might not take long for the Bonettis to figure out he was one of ours."

"Okay, we needed to pull him out. He's gone as far as he could, and he has been undercover for a long time."

When the two senior agents finished talking, Special Agent Monroe left for the day. He hoped tomorrow would bring better news.

Chapter 7

The next afternoon, Gina and Tommy sat in the office talking about the day before. "Are you sore from the brawl last night?" Gina asked.

"A little. Mainly my hand and my eye a little," he said. "Temple got a good shot at my eye. What about you, are you okay?"

"Yeah, Riley and I got a few good shots at each other. How much of the season is left?" Gina asked.

"We are about halfway there," Tommy said.

"You know, I need to go to the store. Why don't you come with me?" Gina said, giving him a concerned look. They decided years earlier that their code to talk somewhere else would be to ask the other to go to the store.

"Sure. Looks like it will be a slow day around here, anyway. We only have one customer coming for two front tires. I'll tell everyone we are heading out for a while," Tommy said.

They drove toward Sully's Irish Pub. Although they didn't go there often, it was the perfect place to talk because the music was loud, and the back corner was dark.

"Looks like someone finally moved that brown van that has been parked out here the last few days," Tommy said.

"It was an eyesore, but do you find it odd that it appeared around the same time Temple came by the store?" Gina said.

"I didn't think of that. Maybe we need to talk to Atlanta again," he said.

They walked into the pub and went directly to a table in the back corner, away from everyone.

Riley opened the bar at noon as usual. Samantha came in tired but excited because Taylor Swift had announced a new double album earlier that morning. After the brawl at the game the night before, Riley hoped for a quiet day.

Around 2:00 p.m., Gina and Tommy walked in and went to the table in the back corner. Riley texted Johnny to let him know they were there. *Lot of nerve coming in here after the fight last night,* she sent.

Johnny texted back that she was to be the one to wait on them. She should treat them like any other customer but let him know if they start anything. *Act as if nothing happened last night,* Johnny sent.

Riley let Samantha know she would take the new table. Samantha was happy because she was trying to read anything she could about the new album on the fan boards. Plus, she wasn't in the mood yet for customers after being up most of the night.

Riley took a deep breath and walked over to Gina and Tommy.

"Hey Riley," Tommy said. "Gina wants a dry martini, and I'll have a Budweiser."

"Sounds good, I'll be back in a minute with your drinks," Riley said and walked back to the bar.

"Do you think we need to be worried about Ricky Temple?" Tommy asked.

"I don't know. It's weird how all this has unfolded," she said.

"He suddenly is the third base coach of Sully's softball team. Then he shows up at the store using a fake name wanting tires. Then a money shipment is intercepted by the highway patrol," Tommy said.

"It's really odd. How much money was in the cases? I have it written down in my book, but I can't remember," Gina asked.

"There was $200k in those cases. I called Atlanta this morning, they are sending a couple more guys up here. The attorney for Neil and Jason was delayed and is now driving up, I'm not sure why. Maybe he had to do something with those hackers. I also told them about the van," Tommy said.

While they were talking, they didn't notice Riley had arrived with their drinks.

"Here you go, guys. Do you need anything else?" Riley asked.

"No. We'll let you know when we need another round," Gina said. "How long was she standing back there?"

"Not sure. I don't think long," Tommy said.

"I'm glad they are sending more people for us. I think we will put them on Temple first thing. Maybe put a scare in him. The attorney being delayed worries me a little. I want to make sure those two guys didn't say anything," Gina said.

Back at the bar, Riley had a text from Johnny wanting to know how it was going and to let her know he was still stuck at his appointment. She was a little rattled. *Why are they talking about Ricky and what suitcases of money? And an attorney from Atlanta, and hackers?* Riley thought. She wondered if she should tell anyone or keep it to herself for now.

She texted Johnny that there hadn't been any problems.

Special Agent Monroe came in late and was just getting to his desk when the watch stander approached.

"Sir, the agents who were on scene last night will be here in about 30 minutes. I also want to let you know that the two suspects left the tire store and went to a local pub a short time ago. A car followed them and is waiting outside for them to exit. Per your direction, we moved the surveillance van out of the area. The wife of one of the local police officers owns a Korean food truck. We arranged to have it parked across the street with an agent inside. The tech department is setting it up with some small listening devices. They are also mounting a camera on the food truck so we can have video. We will set up a rotation between all the agencies just like before. The truck will shut down every night around 8:00 p.m.," the junior agent said.

"Okay, all sounds good. The cover was blown on the first truck. It had only been there for a couple of days. I want to know everything that goes on over there. When those two agents get here, send them right over," Special Agent Monroe said.

"One thing we haven't considered, what if it wasn't Temple and the Feds are onto us?" Gina said to Tommy. "Let's get another round. It's nice in here."

Gina caught Riley's attention and held up two fingers indicating they wanted two more drinks. "I thought of that this morning, too. I still think we are clean. Did you ask Atlanta if they have anything on a federal investigation or anything going on?" Gina asked.

"I did. They are going to look into it, but they haven't heard anything from their sources," Tommy said. He turned to see Riley standing there.

"Here you go. One dry martini and a Budweiser. Anything else?" Riley asked.

"No. I think we'll go ahead and get the check," Tommy said.

After Riley walked away, Tommy looked at Gina with a raised eyebrow.

"She isn't listening. I think she just wants us out of here," Tommy said.

"Well, she's getting her wish. I just got a text from Atlanta. The guys will be at the store in about an hour. I'll pay and then let's get out of here," Gina said.

Twenty minutes later, Gina and Tommy drove the short distance back to the store, with a grey Buick close behind.

"That's cool. Someone put a food truck across the street. That's a good idea," Tommy said.

The two agents who arrested Neil and Jason walked over to their boss, as they had been instructed to do.

"Special Agent Monroe. We were at the vehicle stop last night. We were told you wanted to speak with us," one of the agents said.

"I do, which agency are you from?" he asked.

"I am with the Secret Service, so I was there for the money. He is with DEA and went in case drugs were in the car," one of them said.

"Walk me through it," Special Agent Monroe said.

"Of course. The suspect car departed Tommy's Tire Emporium at 7:00 p.m. I don't think they knew we were following them. As the car approached Concord, NC, we called in to the operations center to get the go ahead to execute the stop," he said.

"Why Concord?" Special Agent Monroe asked. He wanted to understand how they thought.

"It was decided to let them get away from High Point so it would look like a normal traffic stop. It seemed to work well. The first thing they asked the trooper was if they had been speeding. We were right behind them. When we arrived, the two suspects were getting out of the car. One thing of note, one of the troopers said he saw them stomping on their phones as he approached the vehicle," the DEA Agent said. "When we identified ourselves, they immediately asked to call a lawyer and they both stopped talking. My impression was they knew exactly how to act and what to do."

"I understand when you got them to the Cabarrus County Sheriff's Office you separated them immediately. Is that correct? Where are they now?" the senior agent asked. Not everyone knew Neil was an undercover FBI agent, so Special Agent Monroe behaved as if both were suspects.

"Yes sir. They were separated and each given the chance to call an attorney. I believe it was Jason who called an attorney for both of them. Because it was after normal working hours, he had to leave a message with a service. Right now, they are being moved to Federal custody down in Charlotte," the Secret Service Agent said.

"Okay. Good job last night. Let me know if we get anything back from the digital forensic guys on the two cell phones. Have you been briefed yet on the new surveillance?" he asked.

"The food truck, yes sir. One of your guys is on it today and I have it tomorrow. The DEA has the surveillance the next day," the Secret Service Agent said.

Special Agent Monroe waited until they left before turning to his partner. "Anything important from Neil's debriefing? Or should I say, Special Agent Kevin Thomas's debriefing?"

"He gave us a list of places they delivered money to. Apparently, they just started delivering money to some hackers in Greenville, South Carolina. We are adding those locations to our list for when it's time to get search warrants and execute the raids. You wanted us to ask him about the time Temple visited the store. He was there and said Temple came in using the name Tom Hagen and asked about tires. Neil almost laughed because he knew the name he used was from a movie. Tommy and Gina Bonetti were mad about it. That's about it," Special Agent Johnston said.

"Okay. Thanks. Make sure Neil is still in jail when the attorney shows up. We don't want to tip our hand just yet," Special Agent Monroe instructed.

Riley watched Tommy and Gina leave. She was relieved that they hadn't caused a scene. She told Samantha she now had all the tables, and Riley would take care of the bar. Next, she texted Johnny to let him know they had left.

Riley opened the notes app on her phone and typed everything she had heard. Some of it was just partial bits and pieces, but she wanted it to be written down. She put question marks after the things about Ricky, Atlanta, Federal Task Force, and suitcases of money.

After saving her notes, she opened a web browser and typed 'suitcases of money' into the search bar. Several news articles appeared about the stop and arrest in Concord the day before She realized they were all the same information, so she copied the links into her notes and sat down. *What the hell is going on around here?* she thought.

For the next hour she thought about everything she had heard. It seemed like a lot, but when she tried to piece it together, it didn't make sense. She needed to get to the field to warm up for the game against Tucker's Paint.

"Samantha, I'm leaving for the game. It should be quiet until we get back around 7:00. No Taylor Swift, okay?" Riley said.

Ricky and Riley arrived at the game at the same time. They parked next to each other and walked to the field together.

"You ready to pitch another great game tonight?" Ricky asked.

"I guess so," she said. She was still preoccupied with what she had heard at the bar.

"You don't sound like you're too excited tonight. Are you okay?" Ricky asked.

"I'm fine. Tommy and Gina showed up at the bar this afternoon. They don't come in too often, so I thought it was strange, especially after the brawl. They had a couple of drinks and left," Riley said.

Ricky stopped walking and looked at her. She had a look on her face like there was more she wanted to say. They started walking again and joined the rest of the team who were already warming up.

Sully's was the visiting team, so they would bat first. Ricky went to his spot at third base and waited for some action. Riley led off with a single. Ricky noticed she had a look of determination on her face. Next up was Joe B, who flew out to center field. Ricky's action picked up when Juice hit a hard shot to the gap between center and right field. Riley rounded second base, and Ricky held her at third.

"One out, Riley. Go on contact," he said.

That was as far as Riley would get because the next two batters, Gravy and Woody, both flew out: one to the shortstop and the other to the left fielder.

By the third inning, Tucker's Paint had a 3-0 lead. Riley was not pitching a good game. Her head wasn't in it tonight. Ricky thought the determination he saw in the first inning was gone and wondered if their earlier conversation was connected to her bad game.

After a big win against Tommy's Tires, Sully' Pub was having a letdown game. They all knew it was one they should win.

In the sixth inning, Tucker's Paint was ahead 3-0. Sully's started to show some signs of life. Woody led off with a single and moved to second on a base hit by Johnny. Caldwell hit a ball deep into center field. Woody took off from second and Ricky waved him home. Ricky hoped if Woody scored, it would spark the team. It was going to be another close play at the plate, though. Woody started his slide but was a step too slow. Out at home, and the score stayed the same. Otis then hit into a double play that ended the inning.

Sully's never got their offense going and lost the game. After the last out, Ricky called Susan.

"We lost. Now we are tied with Tommy's Tires for first place. Something is up with Riley. She was off all night, and she said that Tommy and Gina were at the pub this afternoon," Ricky said.

"It might have been one of those days. Everyone can't be at their best all the time," Susan said.

"Yeah, but I could tell she wanted to tell me something but held back. Feel like a drink at the pub with the team?" he asked.

"You want me to talk to Riley and see if I can find out what happened?" Susan said.

"And have a drink with me. Yes," Ricky said.

"Okay, I'll be there in about 30 minutes," Susan said.

"Thirty minutes?" Ricky asked.

"I need to get ready and then I'll be down," Susan said. "I'll see you soon," she said. *Click.*

Tommy and the two new guys from Atlanta sat in a rental car parked a few spaces from Ricky's car.

"That's him," Tommy said. "You need to introduce yourselves and persuade him to stay away from the tire store. Talk to him and see if you can get anything out of him. Understand?"

"Yes sir. We'll take care of it," one of them said.

Riley was one of the last people from Sully's team to leave the field. She walked past Tiny's team as they finished warming up before their game. She was moving slowly to her car when something caught her attention. *Is Tommy Bonetti in that car near Ricky? Who are those other two guys with him?* First, they show up at the pub and now she sees him at the ball field.

As she was trying to process what was going on, Tommy's eyes met hers. Riley got nervous so she picked up the pace to her car. She took out her cell phone to make it look like she was on a call. When she got into her car, she added this new information to her notes. While she was typing, the car Tommy was in drove away.

Riley sat there for a few minutes, thinking. She felt sure Tommy Bonetti was not the businessman everyone thought he was, and she was beginning to think he was after Ricky. It never occurred to her that she could become a target as well.

Tommy went home after picking up his car at the tire store. Gina was already there waiting for him. He walked in and grabbed a beer before telling her everything.

"I took the new guys over to the ball field and pointed out Temple. I told them to ask him some questions and let him know to stay away from the store," Tommy said. "One weird thing, after Temple left, I saw Riley leaving. Our eyes locked and she knew I was there. When she saw me, she got nervous and started playing around with her phone."

"This is getting complicated. We have no idea who tipped the police about the money shipment. We don't know what Temple is up to, and we don't know what Riley knows," Gina said.

"It feels like something is going on and we have no idea what it is. Let's see what the guys get out of Temple and then decide what to do next," Tommy said. "The good news is, Sully's lost tonight so we are tied with them now."

"You're worried about softball standings when we have no idea if the police are about to kick down our door? Keep in mind Atlanta said to calm it down," Gina snapped.

"There's nothing we can do now but wait," Tommy said. He could tell by the look on her face that she agreed but didn't like it.

Chapter 8

Ricky woke up and stared out the window at the rain before he jumped in the shower. After drying off and getting dressed, he walked into the kitchen to make coffee while Susan was still waking up. He got two coffee mugs out and then grabbed a cinnamon roll for himself and a chocolate croissant for Susan from the refrigerator. When the coffee was ready, he heard Susan coming down the hallway.

"Perfect timing as usual," he said.

"The rain woke me up. Did you get a croissant out for me?" she asked as she walked into the kitchen. "Did you have another dream last night?"

"Yeah, but it wasn't as bad as they usually are. I think the stress is getting to me. Your croissant is on the counter. I take it you didn't get anything out of Riley last night?" Ricky asked.

Susan took a bite of her breakfast before answering. "No. She told me the same thing she told you and changed the subject to moving to an island. I agree with you, I think she is holding something back."

"I had a feeling you would say that. If she is holding something back, she will tell us when she is ready. I have an appointment this morning but should be home by lunch," Ricky said.

Ricky finished his cinnamon roll and sat with Susan until she was done with breakfast. He changed into some shorts and put on his favorite Top Gun t-shirt. The last thing he did was put on his Red Sox hat.

"I'll let you know when I'm on my way home. See you in a little while," Ricky said.

"While you're gone, I'm going to look through the local news and update the case board in the office. Have a good meeting."

Ricky walked out the front door and down his short driveway to the Cadillac. He was surprised there wasn't a note on it from the HOA. He hoped they had given up.

Since he wasn't sure what he was in the middle of, Ricky decided it was time to be more careful. He checked his tires and then underneath his car for any tracking or other devices. Then he looked under the hood for any obvious signs of tampering. He saw nothing, so he got in and left.

Fifteen minutes later, Ricky was at the medical building. Although he already knew where the office was, he paused to look at the directory, giving himself a chance to collect himself. He walked through the double glass doors, past the elevators to the stairs, and up one flight. He stood in front of Dr. B.F. Pearce's door and took a deep breath before walking in.

"Hi Margaret. I have a 10:00 with Ben," Ricky said.

"Hi Mr. Temple. He is ready for you. Go right in," Margaret said.

"You know, you don't need to call me Mr. Temple. Ricky or Ricky T. works fine for me," he said.

"Okay, Mr. Temple," she replied.

Ricky shrugged, adjusted his Red Sox hat, and opened the door to Ben's office. "Hi Ben. How's it going today?" Ricky said.

"Come on in, Ricky. Take a seat. How are you doing today?" Ben asked.

"I'm doing okay. A lot going on lately. Something is up with Riley. She was acting strange at the game last night," he said, not giving Ben a chance to ask any more questions.

"Who is Riley?" Ben asked.

"We had a brawl at the big game with Tommy's Tires. I got followed by someone," Ricky said, deciding not to mention it was the FBI.

"You were in a brawl?" Ben asked. He tried to keep up with the random thoughts of his new patient.

"Two guys were stopped on I-85 down in Concord. They had suitcases full of money. What is going on around here?" he said. All the things that didn't add up in Ricky's head were coming out of his mouth.

"What about these dreams your wife told me about. Have you had any more of them?" Ben asked.

Ricky sat silent and stared at Ben's diploma from the University of Vermont hanging on the wall. It caught his attention because they are the Catamounts just like Western Carolina, where he and Susan went to college.

"What is that song you keep humming? I noticed it the last time you were here," Dr. Pearce asked.

Ricky didn't realize he was humming out loud. He said, "It's 'Simple Man' by Lynyrd Skynyrd. I really like that song."

"By the way," Ricky said, changing the subject, "Did you hear High Point is getting a soccer team? It's a pro team that will play down where the baseball team plays. You know Ben, I think we've covered a lot of ground today. I'll make an appointment with Margaret on my way out." Ricky stood up and left the office.

"Forty minutes today, Mr. Temple. You do remember that you have a full hour with Ben?" Margaret said.

"He does such a good job, and we accomplish a lot in a short time. Set me up for same time next week please," Ricky said.

Ricky walked out of the office, back down the stairs, and out the double glass doors. He followed the sidewalk around to the right. He had parked on the side of the building under a tree, since it was raining and he never carries an umbrella.

Ricky got his keys out of his pocket and was about to unlock the door when he was grabbed from behind and shoved against his car.

"Why have you been hanging around Tommy's store?" the voice asked.

"What's going on? Who are you? I think you have the wrong guy," Ricky said. He was mad at himself for not feeling the guy behind him.

The guy gave him a hard punch to his kidney. "I asked why you've been hanging around Tommy's?" he asked again.

"Ask me no questions and I'll tell you no lies," Ricky responded.

This was met with another punch to his kidneys. Ricky got the feeling that this guy had done this before. He closed his eyes and took a few deep breaths to calm himself.

He felt the thug grab his shirt and try to throw him against the Caddy. Ricky went on offense and threw his elbow into the guy's stomach as hard as he could. He could tell it had worked because his attacker was bent over, gasping for air. Ricky turned quickly and rammed his foot into the guy's knee as hard as he could. He crumpled to the ground in pain. Ricky grabbed him and rolled him away from the Caddy.

Ricky heard screeching tires coming in his direction fast. He knew it had to be this guy's ride. Ricky got him on his feet and wrapped his hands around his throat.

"You tell Tommy Bonetti that I don't know what's going on, but I'm going to find out. Then I'm coming for him. You tell him!" Ricky yelled only a few inches from the thug's face. Then he pushed him away as the car slammed on its brakes to let him in. Ricky made a mental note of the license plate number as well as the color and model.

With the car out of sight, Ricky picked up his Red Sox hat and got into the car. As he sat behind the wheel, the pain from the kidney punches set in. It didn't help that his eye was bruised and sore from the brawl at the game. He called Susan to let her know what happened and asked her to be ready for him when he got there.

When he pulled into the driveway, he saw Susan had opened the garage door for him. She knew it would be easier for him since there were no steps to contend with to get into the house. It was also closer to the living room where he could collapse on the sofa. Which is what he did.

"What happened? I thought you had an appointment with Dr. Pearce," Susan said.

"I did. He's great. I really like him. When I was leaving, one of Tommy's thugs jumped me in the parking lot," Ricky said.

"You'll be fine. How do you know he works for Tommy?"

"He asked why I was hanging around Tommy's store and told me to stay away," Ricky said. "I gathered myself and got some shots in on him. I think I need to go to the tire store and see if there is a guy limping around. I got a good shot on his knee."

"I know you're pissed off, but I don't think it's a good idea for you to go back down there. Why don't I go?" Susan said.

"You? You don't do operational stuff. I know you helped in Asheville, but that was a one-time thing," Ricky said. "I know you want to help, but the more I think about it the only thing we would gain from you going down there is confirming this guy works for Tommy. I think we already know the answer to that. Let's leave it alone and figure out who owns the car the guy drove off in."

"Okay, write down what you have, and I'll look. It will most likely be a rental, but we might get lucky," Susan said in her dejected voice.

"While you're at it, please take a look at the news again and see if anything new has come out about the arrest down in Concord," Ricky said.

"What are you going to be doing?" Susan asked.

"I'm going to lay here and ice everything that hurts which is most of my body," Ricky said.

"Not sure if you saw the mail, but it's that time again. Your PI license is due for renewal. That was a quick two years." Susan said.

"Ok, I'll take care of it."

The two Atlanta guys drove up to Tommy's Tire Emporium, honked the horn, and waited for one of the service bay doors to open. They pulled in quickly and got out to face an anxious Tommy Bonetti.

"What happened? Why is he limping?" Tommy demanded.

The one who confronted Ricky was about to speak when he saw Gina walking toward them. He didn't want to tell the story twice. When she got to where they were standing, he started.

"I jumped Temple when he came out of a doctor's office. I grabbed him from behind and threw him into that ugly turquoise Cadillac he drives. Once I had him down, I asked why he was coming around here. He just gave some smartass remark, so I punched him a couple of times," he paused to catch his breath. "He threw an elbow in my stomach, and I lost my breath for a second. He kicked my knee hard, and I went down. Then he said to tell you that he's coming for you when he finds out what's going on."

"Temple actually said that he was coming for me?" Tommy asked.

"He did."

Tommy looked at Gina and said, "I need a drink."

"I need to go to the store anyway," Gina said.

Ricky stood up and gingerly walked down the hall. He walked into the office just as Susan was hanging up her phone.

"Did you come up with anything?" he asked.

"Just what we thought," she said. "It's a rental car. They used one of the rental agencies we've worked with before. They wouldn't give me the name but said two guys rented the vehicle yesterday using Georgia driver's licenses. As for the Concord thing, the North Carolina Highway Patrol released a statement this morning. They said the two suspects were stopped for a routine traffic violation when the cases of money were discovered. The two guys are now in Federal custody in Charlotte," Susan said.

"Federal, huh? That means the Secret Service for counterfeiting or money laundering, or it could be the DEA for drug money. Let's not forget about our buddy Chet from the FBI who's in the area too. More pieces of the puzzle."

Chapter 9

Six miles north of RJ Floyd's farm lies Wynot, Nebraska. RJ and his wife Money, as she is called, found a parking space on St. James Avenue right in front of the Devil's Den Bar, their favorite watering hole. RJ had been busy lately and the two needed a change of scenery.

They had increased his cattle from 100 head to 150. With just RJ and Money to look after them, it was a noticeable increase in the workload. On top of that, RJ had accepted another term as the commander of the Veterans group. They were both tired.

They were surprised to see their neighbor at the bar. "Leo, what brings you to town?" Money asked.

They were interrupted by the bartender coming over to get their drink order. "If you got a resupply of New Belgium 1554, I'll take one," RJ said.

"I'll have the same," Money said.

"You're in luck. We got a new supply yesterday. It's good and cold," the bartender said.

"I came in to pick up some supplies and thought I would stop in for a quick beer. What about you two?" Leo said.

"I have a pancake breakfast for my Veterans group this Saturday, so I need to make sure everything is ready," RJ said.

"I'll be there Saturday, but for now I need to get back to the farm. Let me know if you need any help. I know you have a lot going on," Leo said.

"Thanks Leo. I'll stop over after the pancake breakfast and visit," RJ said.

"What do you want to do for dinner?" Money asked.

"You know what I'm going to say. I want your beef bulgogi," RJ said. "Best I've ever had. You need to write down the recipe so I can send it to Ricky. He keeps asking for it."

"I had a feeling you would want that again, so the meat is already marinating. Tell Ricky I make it by feel. It's never the same."

As RJ finished his beer he waved to the bartender for another round. "Forgot to tell you, Dad and Mom are coming this weekend. The Nebraska red and white spring game is on TV, so we are going to watch it together."

"Great, it's almost football season," she said with a laugh.

"No, it's just the spring game so we still have a few months to go," he said.

The bartender brought the second round. RJ picked up his beer to take a drink as his phone rang.

RJ looked at the caller ID and was surprised. He looked at Money and said, "I need to take this."

RJ walked outside to take the call in private. A few minutes later he came back in but didn't sit down.

"Hey," he yelled over to the bartender, "put these on my tab." Then he turned to Money. "We need to go. I need to catch a plane early tomorrow morning. I'll explain on the way home."

Riley opened the door to get some fresh air. The rain was back and coming down hard. She stood in the doorway watching the rain hit the puddles before going back to her spot behind the bar. She put on the Kilkenny's version of 'Galway Girl' and then went back to looking at apartments in the Virgin Islands on her phone.

The door opened and Riley put her phone down. Tommy and Gina walked in, shook off the rain, and went to their usual table in the corner.

Riley texted Johnny to let him know they were back. She then opened her notes app to add that Tommy and Gina were back in the bar and put down the date and time. When that was done, she walked over to see what they wanted.

"Welcome back. Do you two want the same as last time?" Riley asked, trying to keep it casual.

"Sounds good," Gina said. When she was sure that Riley was far enough away, she turned to Tommy. "What do you think about Temple?"

"I don't know but I think we will need to deal with him in some way. If he really said he was coming for me, he either knows what's going on or is figuring it out," Tommy said. He stopped talking when he saw Riley approaching.

"Here you go. A dry martini and a Budweiser. Anything else for now?" Riley asked.

"Go ahead and start another round. It's been a long day," Tommy replied.

For a couple of rounds of drinks, they sat in the corner and listened to music, enjoying not being at the store. Gina thought it was good to do this every so often – blow off steam in the middle of the day and get away from all of life's issues.

Riley could tell that by round number three, Gina and Tommy were starting to feel the effects. Before she went back to their table, she texted Johnny to tell him she wasn't having any issues. While she was happy that her only two customers were behaving themselves, she was equally happy she didn't hear any more talk about Ricky or their business doings.

Soon Tommy was drunk, talking about his union days back in back in New Jersey and its connections to organized crime. When he mentioned Atlanta, it was clear he was starting to slip up. He reminisced with Gina about getting the money to open Tommy's Tire Emporium from 'The Family.' Thinking they were safe because of the dark corner and loud music, Gina started talking too.

"And now I have Temple to worry about," Tommy said before turning to see Riley standing there. He knew she had heard it all. Riley tried to play it off and asked if they wanted the check.

"Yes," Tommy said slurring his words. "How long were you standing there?" he demanded.

"I just walked up," she said, but her eyes and facial expression gave her away. "I'll get your check," she said. Riley hurried back to the bar.

"How much did you think she heard?" Tommy asked Gina.

"I don't know. Let's get out of here," Gina said.

After Riley was sure they were gone, she sat in the empty bar making more notes on her phone. When she was done, she read everything she had heard over the two visits. She didn't know how much was the truth and how much was the alcohol talking. She decided she needed to talk to Ricky as panic set in.

She texted Ricky. *I need to talk to you after practice tomorrow afternoon.* She sent it as Samantha arrived for her shift.

"Samantha, I need to go. I'm not feeling very good. I'll tell Johnny," Riley said. She wanted to get to her apartment to think and stay out of sight.

The next morning, Gina and Tommy were hungover when they arrived late at the tire store. The new guys were waiting by one of the service bays.

"One of you go over to that food truck and see what time it opens. I'm already hungry," Tommy said. He still didn't know their names, but he would learn them later.

Inside the office, Gina watched as Tommy snorted a line. She suggested they go outside to have a quick talk.

"Before you start, I think we have a problem. I can still see the look on Riley's face yesterday. I think she heard a lot more than she needed to," Gina said.

"I was going to say the same thing," Tommy responded. "I know Sully's has a late afternoon practice. Both Temple and Riley should be there. I think we need to grab Riley and find out what she heard. Things are starting to take off for us, and this could be big trouble," he said.

"And do what with her? What about Temple?" Gina asked.

"We'll have them take her to the High Rock Lake house. I can go down there later and question her and stay for the weekend. As for Temple, who cares. They can take care of him at practice. Get him out of the way for good. We just need to make sure we have a story in case the police ask us," Tommy said.

"I need to think about this, kidnapping and murder are big steps," Gina said. They both walked back inside the tire store.

"Hey boss, the truck opens at 11:00," one of the new guys said.

A couple of hours later, Gina told Tommy she agreed with the plan. Tommy walked out to the showroom and brought the new guys outside.

"We have a job for you. It's delicate, but it's what you are here for," Tommy said. "At 6:00 p.m., Sully's Irish Pub is having softball practice at Harvell Park. You two need to be there when they are done. They usually practice for about an hour. You have two people to deal with. The first is a female, Riley Simms," Tommy said. He showed them her picture from the Sully's Pub website. "The other is the guy you met yesterday, Ricky Temple. Take the girl to this address down at High Rock Lake. As for Temple, I don't want to hear about him anymore. Do you understand?" Tommy said. "What are your names again?"

"I'm Jamie and he is Ryan. We understand what you want," Jamie said. He put the address for the lake house into his phone, crumpled up the piece of paper, and threw it toward the trash can, missing. "I want another shot at that Temple guy anyway," Ryan said.

Chapter 10

Ricky woke up from a nap and gathered his things for practice. He was still sore from his unexpected meeting with Tommy's thugs. Susan sat in the office thinking about everything again. She decided that although there was a lot of information, it was only loosely connected so far.

"I'm going to leave a little early and go by the pub. I'm hoping to talk to Riley before practice. After her text wanting to talk, now I know something is up," Ricky said.

"Good. I admit I'm a little anxious about what she has to say," Susan said.

"I was thinking, when this all started you told me that Tommy had a union job up in New Jersey. Am I remembering right?" he asked.

Susan looked at her notes. "Yes, he had a union job right out of high school working on the docks at the international airport."

"While I'm gone, will you see if you can find anything else about the union? The usual stuff, which one he was in and whatever you can find," he asked.

"Yeah, I'll get on it. Are you thinking the union is involved somehow?" she asked.

"Who knows, but it's a possibility we shouldn't overlook. Anyway, I'm heading out and will let you know as soon as I talk to Riley," Ricky said. He walked out of the office, grabbed his keys, put on his Red Sox hat, and headed for Sully's Irish Pub.

When he arrived, he knew immediately he wouldn't be talking to Riley before practice. She wasn't there. Ricky had a few minutes to kill before practice, so he got a beer. He asked Samantha for a Miller High Life.

Samantha opened the beer cooler to look for it. She moved bottles and cans around looking at all the labels before she finally gave up.

"Sorry sir, it seems we are sold out of Miller High Life, is there something else I can get you?" she asked.

"Sure, how about Sam Boston?" Ricky said.

"Okay just give me a second," Samantha said. She dove back into the beer cooler, this time looking for Sam Boston. She found one and opened it for him.

Ricky sipped his beer while looking around the bar, trying to piece together the puzzle in his mind. He was finishing his beer when his phone rang. It was Susan.

"No, I haven't talked with Riley yet," Ricky said as he answered.

"It's not that. The HOA is suing us because you parked the Caddy on the street and ignored the fines," Susan said.

He could hear the anger in her voice. "These idiots think they have so much power. With everything else going on, we don't need this too," Susan complained.

"I know," he said trying to be calm. "We'll talk about it when I get home. Don't worry too much," Ricky said. He hung up, put his empty beer bottle on the counter, and left for practice.

When Ricky got to the field, he scanned the area to make sure nothing looked out of place. Too much had gone on for him to let his guard down. Satisfied, he went to join his team.

"Let's go, everyone. Last practice of the year, unless we get to the playoffs, so let's look good," Johnny said. "Ricky, do your usual with the infield and work on double plays."

"You got it, Johnny," Ricky said. He looked at Riley who was over on the first base side throwing a few pitches. Their eyes met. Ricky grabbed a bat and ball and started working with the infield as Johnny had asked.

After an hour, Johnny called everyone in. "Did everyone get a chance to take a few swings for batting practice?" he asked.

A few of the guys said yes but most just nodded their heads.

"Good. As you know, our last game is tomorrow night against Tiny's. If the standings stay the way they are now, we will be moving on to the Regionals with a chance at going to Asheville for the Championships. I'll keep an eye on the score of the Tommy's Tires and Tucker's Paint game. If we win and Tommy's loses, then we win the league. I'll send a text. Ricky and Riley, it's your turn to clean up. We'll see you guys at the pub shortly."

The team walked off the field and went to their cars for the short drive over to the pub. Ricky started collecting the bats and helmets as Riley walked around the field gathering up the balls.

Ricky looked up and saw that the parking lot was empty and was surprised another team wasn't practicing after them. The sun was starting to go down when Riley walked into the dugout where Ricky was waiting for her.

"I asked Johnny to have us clean up today. Hope you don't mind," Riley said.

"So, what did you want to talk about?" Ricky asked.

"Let's talk on the way to the car," Riley said.

As Ricky walked out of the dugout, he heard the unmistakable sound of a gunshot. Instinctively, he dropped to the ground, pulling Riley down with him. More shots rang out.

Ricky turned and saw the shock on Riley's face. The dugout was only a few feet away and made of concrete blocks. "We need to get to the dugout. Do you understand me?" he yelled.

"Yes," she said shakily.

Ricky needed to figure out where the shooters were before getting the two of them out of there. He felt sure they were somewhere near the parking lot. He stood at the edge of the dugout with the parking lot on his left, about 40 yards away. He saw a couple of trees close to him, and he decided to make a move for them. He wanted a better look and to draw their fire away from Riley.

"Get down on the ground and make yourself as small as you can. I'll be back to get you. Don't leave here till I come get you" Ricky told her. He didn't wait for a reply and moved back to the edge of the dugout for a better view.

Ricky broke from the dugout and ran for the trees. As soon as he stepped out, they started shooting again. Ricky got to the trees without being hit and let out a relieved breath. He guessed there were two shooters. One was at a 45-degree angle to his left, and the other was at the same angle to the right.

He poked his head out to confirm his guess. As soon as he did, multiple shots hit the trees. He was pinned down. Ricky wasn't convinced he could make it back to the dugout. He took a quick look to make sure Riley was on the ground. He was happy to see she had listened to him and was on the ground in a ball. It was slowly getting darker, and Ricky wished for sunset to hurry up.

He got down on his belly and started to crawl back toward the dugout. As soon as he was barely away from the trees, gunfire broke out. Ricky hoped someone would hear the gunshots and called the police. It might be his only hope.

Ricky waited another couple of seconds and stuck his head out again. He was greeted with another burst of gunfire, but something was different this time. Ricky swore there were three shooters now. The third one was shooting differently than the original two, in controlled two-round bursts.

Ricky heard a thud behind him. He turned in a panic thinking someone was coming up behind him. He only saw a 9mm lying beside him. Ricky picked it up. It had a full 15 round magazine, so he charged the gun, putting a round in the chamber. Then he heard two clanks beside him. He turned again to see two full magazines on the ground. Then he heard, "On me."

Ricky dropped his head and smiled. He recognized the voice. He jumped up, took his newly acquired gun off safe and joined the third shooter as he walked up toward him. They got in a line with about five yards between them and started walking and firing at the shooters in the parking lot. After they had moved several yards toward the parking lot, Ricky heard, "Reloading," as his new partner dropped a magazine and loaded another within seconds.

Next, they heard police sirens and the screeching of tires. Ricky put his gun on safe, turned, and said, "RJ Floyd what the hell are you doing here?"

"Apparently, I'm getting arrested with you," RJ said with a smirk.

"Drop your weapons and get down on your knees. NOW," the first High Point Police officer yelled.

RJ and Ricky looked around and saw at least five police officers with their guns pointed at them. They both dropped their guns and got down on their knees as they were told. Two officers approached them while the others covered their movement. Ricky and RJ were handcuffed, picked up, and walked quickly to the back of one of the police cars.

On the way to the patrol car, Ricky said to the officer, "Go down and look in the…"

"Be quiet! You two have done enough for one night. You'll have your chance to talk to the magistrate later," the officer said.

When they got into the patrol car, one of the officers sat in the front seat to keep an eye on them.

"So, how's it going?" Ricky asked.

"Good. It seems to be a little warmer here than in Nebraska," RJ replied.

"How's everything on the farm? How many head of cattle do you have now?" Ricky asked.

"The farm is good. We have 150 head now," RJ said.

One of the policemen yelled for the patrolman in the car with RJ and Ricky. He got out of the car and walked over to see how he could help.

As soon as the door closed, RJ yelled, "WHY THE HELL DIDN'T YOU CALL ME AND TELL ME YOU NEEDED HELP? INSTEAD, SUSAN HAD TO CALL."

"SUSAN TOLD ON ME? PLUS, I DIDN'T KNOW I NEEDED HELP. I WAS STILL FIGURING EVERYTHING OUT," Ricky yelled back.

"YOU HAVE AN ORGANIZED CRIME SYNDICATE AFTER YOU. I SAW THE BOARD IN THE OFFICE AT THE CONDO," RJ continued yelling.

The patrolman came back and stared at them for a second before turning his attention back to the report he needed to fill out.

"How's Jerry and Sandy?" Ricky asked.

"Dad and Mom are doing well," RJ replied.

"And what about Money?"

"Same. She is doing good. She'll be pissed when I tell her about this, but she is good for now," RJ said.

The patrolman in the car was again called out to help photograph the scene. As he walked away, he looked over his shoulder at his two prisoners.

"AT LEAST THIS TIME YOU CALLED OUT WHEN YOU WERE RELOADING. UNLIKE THAT TIME IN TIKRIT WHEN I SUDDENLY FOUND MYSELF TO BE THE ONLY ONE SHOOTING," Ricky yelled. "AT LEAST THAT FBI HOSTAGE RESCUE GUY KEPT SHOOTING WITH ME."

Ricky turned to look at his army buddy and they laughed. "It's good to see you brother," Ricky said.

"It's good to see you too, brother," RJ said. "What's next?"

"I assume we will be brought downtown and booked. I'll call Susan to find an attorney and get us out as soon as she can," Ricky said.

A few hours later, Ricky and RJ Floyd sat in adjoining jail cells waiting for Susan to show up or to get pulled out of the cell for a court appearance. They both had used their phone call and now it was a waiting game. They knew better than to talk business until they got out.

Susan heard a knock at the door and rushed out of the office to answer it. She was relieved to see Father Tim Daniels standing there. She was afraid it was someone from the HOA.

"It's so good to see you," she told him as she gave him a big hug. "We've got a problem, and I think we need your other hat again. I have a check ready for you as a retainer. Come on in, there's a lot going on."

"Slow down, Susan. You said on the phone the HOA was suing you guys, and you wanted to talk about it. It's nothing to get this worked up about," Father Tim said.

"Something else has happened. Come back to the office," she said, gesturing toward the hallway. "After we got off the phone, my police scanner went crazy. There was a gun fight at one of the parks in town. Ricky and RJ were involved and were arrested," Susan explained.

"RJ is in town?" he asked. As he waited for more information, Father Tim looked at Susan's board that held the details of the case.

"Yes. Ricky didn't call him for help this time, so I did. He flew into Greensboro and arrived after Ricky left for softball practice." Susan took a couple of minutes and explained what she could while Father Tim listened.

"We need to get to the police department," he said. "Was anybody hurt?"

"It didn't sound like it, and no ambulance responded," Susan said. She ran down the hall to get her keys.

"I'll drive," Father Tim said, "You can fill me in more on the way."

Ricky and RJ sat in their cells, talking about old times. They were beginning to think they would be there all night. The last time they saw a clock, it was after midnight.

They heard the door open and footsteps coming down the walkway.

"Temple and Floyd, get up. You've been sprung," one of the guards said.

Ricky and RJ got up as fast as they could. They didn't want to give him a chance to change his mind. One guard opened the door and the four of them walked down the hallway, with one guard behind them and another leading them. They stopped at a counter to get their belongings. Ricky and RJ took their time to make sure everything the police took when they were booked was returned to them. It always took longer than expected to get out of jail. When they were finally done, they were told to see the officer at the desk before leaving.

Ricky and RJ walked through the door and saw Susan pacing around the waiting area.

"Good job. You got here fast," Ricky said to Susan.

"How are you two out already? We haven't done anything yet," she said.

"We? Who were you able to get down here at this time of the morning?" Ricky asked. He turned to see Father Tim Daniels walking over.

The two embraced and then RJ hugged him as well.

"I don't know how you two are out, but I think we need to get out of here before they change their minds," Tim said.

Everyone but Ricky started toward the door. Susan stopped and looked back at him.

"Come on. What are you waiting for?" Susan asked.

"Riley," Ricky said. "Where is she? She was with me at the shootout. I put her in the dugout and told her not to leave. I tried to tell them at the scene, but they didn't want to listen to me."

Ricky walked over to the policeman at the main desk. Ricky knew him so he felt he could get some answers.

"Hey Phil. What happened to Riley Simms?" he asked.

"Ricky. You need to get out of here. There are a lot of people who are not happy that you two were released. I don't know anything about Riley Simms," Phil answered.

"You have to, she was there tonight too. She was in the dugout. Pull up the report and see if she is mentioned," he said.

"Okay hold on while I find it. No. No mention of a Riley Simms or any female being involved. Ha, now that's cool," Phil said.

"What. What are you seeing?" Ricky asked.

"The other guy with you is named RJ Floyd."

"Yeah. So what?" Ricky said.

"I wonder if anyone ever calls him RJ 'Pink' Floyd or something like that. He's got a built-in nickname," the officer said.

"Nobody calls him Pink Floyd or anything like that. Focus, Phil. Look at the report one more time and make sure there is no mention of a female named Riley Simms," Ricky said.

"Nothing. Sorry Ricky. That will be $20 for the report though," Phil said.

"I don't want a copy of the report. I just wanted you to read it to me. I'm not paying," Ricky said.

"I almost forgot. I was supposed to give you this when you got out and let you know we will be keeping the two guns," Phil said.

"That's okay, I have other guns," Ricky said. He took the sealed envelope, put it in his pocket, and walked over to join the others. All four of them walked out of the police station.

Ricky turned to RJ and said, "That was crazy. I can't imagine anyone calling you Pink Floyd."

"No kidding. What's the plan?" RJ asked.

"Susan, can you call Johnny and get Riley's address? And then try to call her. RJ and I need to go back to the park and take a quick look around. We need to get our cars too. Let's all meet up at the Coffee Bar. By the time we are done they should be open," Ricky said.

"I'll stay with Susan," Father Tim said.

They all crammed into the Ford Escape for the short ride to the park. Nobody noticed the car following them. When they got to the park, RJ and Ricky walked down to the dugout where Ricky had last seen Riley.

"I was standing right here when they started shooting at us. We both went to the dugout for cover. I told Riley to lie down and get as small as she could and to stay put until I got back. You know the rest," Ricky said.

RJ and Ricky looked around the dugout when they heard a cell phone ringing. The sky was starting to get brighter, but it was still dark enough that they could see the light of the phone. Ricky walked over and picked it up.

"It's Riley's phone," Ricky said.

"Are you sure?"

"Yeah, Susan is calling it now," Ricky said.

Ricky didn't answer it. Instead, he called Susan on his own phone and told her what they had found. Susan gave him Riley's address. Ricky said he and RJ would go over there. They agreed to leave RJ's rental car at the park for now. As they walked to the Cadillac, Ricky noticed Riley's car was still in the parking lot.

It was short ride to Riley's apartment. RJ got out first, looked around, and didn't notice anything out of the ordinary. They both walked up to the apartment number and knocked. No answer. They knocked several more times in case she was in the shower or asleep, but there was still no answer. Ricky walked around the side to try and look through a window while RJ went to the back to look through the patio door. There was no sign of Riley, so Ricky and RJ decided to join the others.

It was now almost 7:00 a.m., so the coffee shop was open. RJ and Ricky walked in and saw Susan and Tim at a table in the back. Thankfully, they had already ordered coffee for everyone. Susan put down her croissant as Ricky walked up. "I wasn't the target," he said. "Riley is missing."

It took Ryan 45 minutes to drive from the park in High Point to the house on High Rock Lake, south of Lexington. He and Jamie were tired and worried. They knew Tommy would be pissed off that they had missed Temple. They would have to deal with that later.

Ryan parked as close to the side entrance as he possibly could and got out. He opened the rear door, grabbed Riley, and yanked her out of the car. Jamie opened the door to a room as Ryan shoved Riley into the room beside the garage.

Riley had been crying uncontrollably since they grabbed her. While they were shooting at Temple, Jamie sneaked down to the other side of the dugout and waited for Temple to make his move. When Temple moved away from the dugout, Jamie put a gag on the girl and brought her up to the car. Temple couldn't hear her screaming for him over the gunfire. Once she was in the car, they sped off before the police arrived.

Ryan threw her on the couch and tied her legs and hands together. They walked out, leaving Jamie to stand guard in case she got brave and figured out a way to escape. Ryan went to make the phone call to Tommy he didn't want to make.

Sitting in the back of the coffee shop, the four friends talked through what they knew. They finished their first coffees quickly and were waiting for refills.

"I assumed they were trying to assassinate me," Ricky said as they settled into cup number two. "We need to get some rest. I don't think RJ has slept for two days. He had an early flight down here and immediately got into a fire fight and then arrested."

"Don't you think 'assassinate' is a bit dramatic?" Susan asked.

"No, I don't. I can see the headlines in the newspaper now. Big bold black letters that say, 'Ricky T Assassinated,'" Ricky said.

"Moving on. What was in that envelope the police gave you?" Tim asked.

"Good question. I forgot all about it," Ricky said as he pulled it out of his pocket. He opened it and started to read.

"Well, my good friend Chet is the one who got us out. Chet is an FBI agent who questioned Susan a few days ago. I met with him as well," Ricky said, explaining to RJ and Father Tim. "It says I need to call him before noon today to set up a meeting or he will send agents for me. I'll call him and get it over with."

Ricky picked up his phone and dialed the number. "Mr. PI. I was wondering when we would hear from you. Are you enjoying your coffee?" Special Agent Monroe said.

"It's private investigator. Thanks for getting us out of jail, Chet. I assume we owe you something in return," he said. Ricky listened as Chet spoke. He turned and looked out the front window of the coffee shop. "I see it. We'll see you soon," Ricky said. *Click.*

"What's up?" RJ asked.

"Chet wants to see us. All of us. That black Suburban parked outside will take us to him. They've been following us since we left the police station," Ricky said. "Sleep will have to wait a little longer."

As they walked out of the coffee shop, two agents got out of the Suburban and opened the doors for them to get in.

The agent took a side street to the post office that passed behind Sully's Pub. Ricky looked to see if Riley's car was there, hoping they had just missed her at the park and her apartment. There was still no sign of her. They pulled into the back parking lot of the High Point Post Office.

When they were out of the Suburban, Ricky leaned over to RJ and said, "We're at the Post Office. Federal. I think we are about to find out what we are in the middle of."

The agent led them up the ramp, past the loading docks, and to a stairwell. Susan and Tim looked uncomfortable as they followed the agent down one flight of stairs and into the Task Force Command Center.

Susan saw signs for the DEA, Secret Service, and High Point Police Department. They walked toward four desks in the center of the room. Behind all the desks was an area with large TV screens and radios.

As they walked through the desks, someone yelled, "RICKY T.? RJ FLOYD?" Ricky and RJ turned to see someone coming toward them. "I haven't seen you two since Tikrit."

"Holy crap. Paul?" Ricky and RJ said at the same time.

"Yeah, it's me. I heard two locals got in a shootout last night but had no idea it was you two," Special Agent Paul Adams said.

"Let me introduce ourselves. I'm Ricky Local and this is RJ Local," Ricky said, laughing.

"If I had known you were in the area, I would have guessed you two were involved," Paul said.

"Paul, this is my wife Susan, and this is Father Tim Daniels," Ricky said as he turned toward Susan and Tim. "This is Paul Adams. He was on the FBI HRT and was with RJ and me in Tikrit one time," Ricky said. He turned back to Paul, "We are here to meet with Chet. He's a fun guy."

"He isn't too bad. He's a bit cranky these days because he is six months from turning 57. I'm still with HRT, if that tells you something," Paul said. "Here's my card with my cell number but I better let you get over to Special Agent Monroe."

"Have a seat. That includes you, Tom Hagen. You two had quite the night, didn't you?" Special Agent Monroe said as the foursome arrived at his desk.

"You have a nice Task Force going here. Looks like you have all the players to go against organized crime," Ricky said. "I take it Tommy Bonetti is connected in some way?"

"I wouldn't disagree with that statement," Special Agent Monroe said. "What can you tell me that I don't already know?"

"We don't know what you know, so I have no idea what to tell you," Ricky replied.

"I will tell you that your assumptions are correct. Now tell me what I don't know," Special Agent Monroe said again.

"Our friend, Riley Simms, is missing. She was with me last night when Tommy's goons tried to kill me. I assume you will be adding that to his charges," Ricky said.

"Walk me through last night," Monroe said.

"We had just finished practice. Riley and I stayed behind to clean up. We were getting ready to leave when they started shooting at us. I decided to move to a clump of trees to try and get a better angle to see who it was. I told Riley to stay in the dugout. I got pinned down. I hoped to get to my car and drive down to the dugout to get Riley. But like I said, I got pinned down," Ricky said.

"I heard the shots when I pulled into the parking lot," RJ said. "I saw Ricky behind the tree. I grabbed the two guns I had gotten from Ricky's house along with some extra ammo. Then I gave him some cover fire. When I got close enough to Ricky, I tossed him one of his guns and we got in line and walked our fire in on the two shooters. I had to reload and called out I was reloading." RJ looked at Ricky. "That's when they took off. The local cops came in from the other side, and you know the rest."

"Why would they come after you?" Special Agent Monroe asked.

"That's the million-dollar question, Chet. I have no idea what I'm in the middle of," Ricky said.

"What about you two?" Special Agent Monroe said, pointing to Susan and Father Tim.

"You already met my wife. This is Father Tim Daniels. He is the attorney for all three of us," Ricky said.

"Of course you have a priest as your lawyer. Anything else you can tell me?" Special Agent Monroe asked.

"Maybe I missed it, but I didn't hear a reply about the attempted murder charges for them trying to kill RJ and Ricky. There is also the matter of what appears to be a kidnapping," Father Tim said. "When do you expect to bring these charges?"

"We have our hands full at the moment, but I assure you we are looking into all of it, Father," Special Agent Monroe said.

"Chet, I assure you I'm not assured," Ricky said. "Finding Riley should be top priority. So, if there is nothing else, we need to look for our friend and need a ride back to our cars."

"You four stay out of this. Let us do our job," Special Agent Monroe said.

He waved to the agent who had driven them to the Command Center to let him know the guests were ready to leave.

Back at the coffee shop, Susan asked, "What is so important about an FBI agent turning 57?"

"The FBI has mandatory retirement for their agents when they turn 57. A lot of them hate it and get bad attitudes. They feel like they are just getting into their prime and have a lot of productive years left," Ricky said.

"What was that Tom Hagen thing?" Father Tim asked.

"Oh, I went to Tommy's Tire Emporium the other day and that's the name I used. It's interesting that he knew that."

The four were tired. They got back to the condo and everyone but Ricky crashed. He had to call Johnny Sullivan. The last game of the season was scheduled for later that evening. After explaining the situation to Johnny, he emphasized to him he couldn't tell anyone about any of it. Then Ricky went to sleep.

Chapter 11

Tommy was annoyed when he got to the lake house. He told the guys he wanted Temple dead and the girl to be taken to the lake house so he could question her. They could only handle half of the assignment. He opened the door to the room inside the garage and looked at Riley. She was still tied up on the sofa.

"WAKE UP," he yelled at her.

Riley started to cry again. She had managed to calm herself down a couple of hours after they threw her into the room. She was sore and could feel bruises forming on her arm and leg from where the two guys had been not so gentle.

"What did you hear me and Gina talking about?" Tommy demanded.

"I didn't hear anything," Riley said, sobbing.

She didn't notice Ryan had come up beside her. Tommy looked at him and nodded.

Ryan slapped Riley hard across the face. Her head jerked backward, causing her to hit her head on the back of the sofa.

"What did you hear Gina and I say in the pub?" Tommy asked again.

She didn't answer. She couldn't stop crying and couldn't calm down.

"Stop crying and answer the question," he said.

"I didn't hear anything. I promise," Riley finally said.

"Who are you working for?" Tommy asked.

"You know I work for Johnny Sullivan," she managed to say.

Tommy nodded to Ryan again. Another slap came across her face. Riley could feel the swelling around her eye as her vision started to blur.

"I saw the look on your face the other day. I know you heard something," Tommy said. He jerked her head up, so she had to look into his eyes. "I'm not playing anymore. This is your last chance to answer my question or I'm going to let Ryan loose." He threw her head down, gave Ryan a nod, and walked out of the room.

Walking away toward the main house, Tommy heard Riley's screams. Next time he would have her brought to him. But for now, she needs to feel pain for a while.

"You two idiots go back to High Point and stay with the store. When you close tomorrow, come back down here. Can you do that without screwing it up?" Tommy said over his shoulder.

"You can count on us, boss," Ryan said.

It was 3:00 p.m. when everyone woke up. They all wanted more sleep but knew they needed to find Riley. Ricky and RJ talked through what they knew, which wasn't much. Just as Father Tim was about to leave to visit his uncle, Susan came into the living room with some information.

"Ricky asked me to look into the union Tommy Bonetti was in when he lived in New Jersey," she said to RJ and Tim. "About 10 years ago there was an investigation into the union head. He was suspected of having connections with the Bellini crime family based out of Newark. The case was dropped but would you like to guess who the lead agent was?" she asked the group.

"Who?" Ricky asked.

"Special Agent Chester Monroe of the FBI," Susan said.

"Well, that explains why he is here. Trying to finish something he started years ago. Tim, I know you need to get to your uncle's for a visit but if you have a couple of minutes I have a few ideas," Ricky said.

"The visit can wait. What are you thinking?" Father Tim asked.

"You all know I need to leave in about an hour for our last softball game," Ricky said to RJ and Tim. "Father Tim, we are going into a grey area again."

"Same as before. I support you guys and understand that at times you have to do things your own way. The fact is, there is a young woman missing and we need to bring her home where she belongs. I'll help you however I can," Father Tim said.

"Thanks. Late tonight after the game, RJ and I will visit Tommy's Tire Emporium. We'll look around and see what we can find out. You good with that, RJ?" Ricky asked.

"Sounds good to me. Are you thinking about putting in some bugs or tagging some cars like last time?" RJ asked.

"I think we bring them, but more importantly let's be ready to take pictures of anything we find. If we find anything important, we will turn it over to Chet, eventually. Susan will show you the building on her map and the sketch I drew when I was there. Develop a plan and we can take off around 1:00 a.m.," Ricky said. "We've done this before so not much will change. RJ and I will do the entry, and Susan will be here on the phone with us listening to the police scanner for any troubles. Tim, we will need you to be on standby in case it all goes bad."

"I will have my phone on all night. If I don't get a call, then I will assume it went well and meet you guys tomorrow for lunch. Have you ever been to the Dog House?" Father Tim said. "It's a local institution."

"I've heard of it, but have never been because it's always so busy," Susan said.

"We can use the back door like all the other locals," Father Tim said.

Tim left, RJ and Susan got to work, and Ricky napped for a few minutes before he had to go to the game.

At the last possible minute, Ricky woke up and got his gear ready. He walked into the office where RJ was analyzing Tommy's Tire Emporium. "What do you think?" Ricky asked.

"I'm just getting started, but I think we'll go in the door by the service bays. Looks like there might be a little concealment from the main road there. Susan is taking me to pick up my car and then I'll drive by," RJ said.

"Sounds good. I should be back here by 8:00 p.m. I'm leaving a few minutes early to make sure Johnny doesn't say anything to the team. I also want to see who is filling in for Riley," Ricky said. "I'll see you tonight."

When Ricky got to the ballpark, he saw Johnny walking down to the field. "Hey Johnny, wait up!" Ricky yelled.

"Hey Ricky. Anything new on Riley?" Johnny asked.

"No, not yet. We are working on it. Did you already tell the team that she is sick and can't play tonight?" Ricky asked.

"Yeah, I told them. I got Samantha pitching tonight. What about the police? Are they doing anything?" Johnny asked.

"I'm sure they are, but I'm taking this personally. I have some friends in town, and we are going to find her and bring her home. I promise," Ricky said.

"What about her parents?" Johnny asked.

"I always got the impression she doesn't have much of a relationship with them," Ricky said.

Johnny and Ricky walked down to meet the team. As they got closer, they put on their happy faces.

"Last game, everyone," Johnny said. "Most of you should know Samantha from the pub, but if you don't, make sure you introduce yourselves. She will fill in for Riley while she is sick. Let's lock in on defense and have some fun tonight. We are the visiting team, so we bat first. Ricky, head over to third base and get us some runs."

Ricky thought Johnny laid it on a little thick but at least he didn't say 'let's win this for Riley who is missing, and we think might be kidnapped.' Ricky trotted over to his spot as Samantha got ready to bat. She hadn't played in a while, and it showed. She grounded out to the pitcher, but the entire team cheered for her anyway. Joe B continued his hitting streak and ripped a double to deep right field. As Joe B approached second base, Ricky gave him the hold sign and pointed to where the ball was. He wasn't there long because Juice hit a long single to left field and Ricky waved Joe B home. Sully's took a 1-0 lead in the first.

It wasn't much of a game. The combination of Sully's playing well and Tiny's team knowing they weren't going to the playoffs made it lopsided. Otis and Woody made great defensive plays while Caldwell, Johnny, and Gravy hit the ball well. By the third inning, the score was 8-0. If Sully's scored two more runs, the game would end because of the mercy rule.

Ricky sent everyone he could around third to home plate. Not only did he want to end a game that wasn't in doubt, but he also wanted to get home and get the night's real work underway. By the end of the fifth inning, it was over. Sully's won 14-0 as the umpire called the game.

"Great game, everyone! Thanks to Samantha for pitching. With this win we are guaranteed a spot in the playoffs. As soon as I get the info, I'll send it out over the team text. A little will depend on the outcome of the next game, Tommy's Tires vs. Tucker's Paint," Johnny said. "As usual, you all get free beer for having such a good season. I'll see everyone at the pub."

"Johnny, I'm heading home. I have some work to do. I'll let you know when we have progress on Riley," Ricky said.

Ricky walked up the hill toward his car. He felt anxious and guilty about Riley's disappearance. *I was with her the other night, and I didn't protect her. I never thought they would go after her. But they did. Why?*

Ricky was back at the condo at 7:30 p.m. He told Susan and RJ about the game. He knew they didn't really care, but he wanted to get it out of his system before they settled into the work ahead. He wanted a beer but knew that he would have to wait. He chugged down some water instead. The three went to the office to go over the plan.

"I drove by Tommy's Tires a little while ago," RJ said. "I hung out across the street at the laundromat. There was a Korean food truck there, so I got some food to try to blend in. Not as good as Money's but it was okay. I think the food truck might be surveillance. There were a few antennas that didn't fit and one of the guys in the truck looked familiar from our visit to the post office."

"Is the food truck going to be a problem?" Ricky asked.

"No, I asked what time they closed. He said 8:00 p.m. He might have recognized me but I'm not sure. Mainly I think we need to be aware that there may already be bugs in the building," RJ said.

"Okay, I think we still bring all our equipment and figure it out as we go. I guess noise discipline will be important until we figure out what we are dealing with," Ricky said.

"No change to what we talked about earlier. The problem is the area around the target building is wide open. There is no cover. We will still go in the back door as we discussed," RJ said. "One option is to use the parking lot behind the building. There are a couple of large clumps of trees we can park in and then use as cover to get to the back of the building. We may just need to leave a little early and go with what feels right."

"I agree. I noticed the parking lot and trees when the FBI was chasing me around last week. I think that is our primary point. The secondary choice may be the laundromat across the street," Ricky said. "We leave at 1:00 a.m. and it's about 15 minutes to our primary insertion point. If we run into the police or some of Chet's gang, we head for the highway."

"Sounds good," RJ said.

"Susan, do you have any questions?" Ricky asked.

"No. I assume you want the usual from me. I'll be on the call and will write down everything you do so we have a record. I'll also listen to the police scanner. If there is any sign of trouble, I'll let you know and call Tim," she said.

"Perfect. We will also need you to let us know how long we have been inside. Start the clock when I tell you we are entering. Let's try to get a little rest before we get ready to leave," Ricky said. "Also, Susan, can you charge Riley's phone and play around with it to see if you can figure out her passcode? Try to think like her."

"Already started on it," Susan said.

The three of them got a couple of hours of sleep. Ricky was the first up and made a pot of coffee. RJ got up next and joined Ricky in the kitchen.

"Did you ever do anything about your dreams?" RJ asked.

"Susan found me a great doctor. I've been seeing him," Ricky said.

"But is it helping any?" he asked.

"It's early but I do feel better and was sleeping a little better before Riley went missing," Ricky said.

They heard Susan stirring in the bedroom, so Ricky got another coffee mug and poured her a cup. The pot was empty, so they brewed another. It was almost ready when Susan appeared in the kitchen and joined the guys.

"Are you still leaving at 1:00?" she asked as she pulled a bagel out of the refrigerator.

"We are. We were just about to go put the equipment in some backpacks and make sure we have extra ammo in case we are surprised by Tommy's goons," Ricky said. "I don't think we should go anywhere without a gun until this is over. They've already proven they will shoot, so we need to be ready to shoot back."

A little before 1:00, Ricky and RJ walked through the garage and placed their backpacks in the back seat of RJ's rental car. They got in and tested their earpieces. With all their checks complete, RJ backed down the driveway, and they left.

Ricky put on some Evanescence and cranked it up. The adrenaline was kicking in along with the caffeine from the coffee. It only took 10 minutes to get to the parking lot instead of the 15 minutes they had planned. RJ parked as far under the trees as he could. They got out and grabbed their gear. Ricky wished he had brought his Red Sox hat. He felt naked without it.

"Base, we are parked and moving to a clump of trees," Ricky said.

"I got it," Susan said as she wrote it down and noted the time.

Ricky and RJ knelt at the base of a tree, listening. They wanted to make sure nobody else was around. RJ had determined it was about 225 feet from where they parked to end of the trees. Then another

75 feet out in the open to the door. Although they were still under the cover of the trees, they moved slowly and as quietly as possible.

"We are at the edge of the trees. We will move to the door in a couple of minutes," Ricky said.

"Copy all," Susan said.

Ricky pulled his lock pick kit out of his pack so he would have it ready. Then he tapped RJ on the shoulder indicating he was ready to move. There would be no more talking until they were back in the car.

RJ moved to the edge of the building and around the corner to the door with Ricky close behind. RJ pulled his gun. Ricky pulled his lock pick and got to work while RJ kept watch. Ricky was surprised the deadbolt was not locked, just the door lock. That saved him some time. He heard the lock pop open and took a deep breath before turning the handle, not knowing if they had an alarm.

"Entering now," he said.

"Copy, starting the clock and be careful," Susan replied.

Ricky turned the handle and opened the door. No alarm. They entered the service bays as fast as they could. RJ closed the door behind them as Ricky got his bearings. He saw the door leading to Tommy's office and walked toward it. When he got to the office door he tried turning the handle, but it was locked. Ricky made quick work of the lock on the office door. They walked in, closing it behind them.

Ricky went to the desk while RJ went to the filing cabinets. Ricky walked around the corner of the desk and sat down. He turned the computer on and was prompted to enter a password. He turned the keyboard over and saw a piece of paper with what looked like a password written on it.

"Guys, you've been inside for five minutes," Susan said. She could barely hear the whispered acknowledgement.

As Ricky was about to type the password, RJ walked toward him. He got as close as he could and whispered in Ricky's ear, "bugs." Ricky gave him a thumbs up and went back to the computer. He looked through files and programs until he found the inventory and accounting information. Knowing he couldn't use the printer, he took out his phone and took pictures of all the screens so they could analyze it later. When he was done, he closed everything out and logged off.

Ricky stood up and quietly moved the chair back so he could stand behind the desk and look around the office. He knew there were more microphones somewhere and he watched as RJ made a sweep of the office. Ricky heard a different sound from the floor as he took a step. He looked down at the small rug the chair had been on and bent down to move it. A door.

"Guys, you've been inside for nine minutes," Susan said.

"Copy," RJ whispered.

Ricky walked over to RJ whispered, "Trap door under the desk."

RJ gave him a thumbs up and they moved to the trap door. RJ took his phone out to take pictures while Ricky worked the lock. He opened it and pulled the door up as quietly as he could. As Ricky started down the short ladder, he noticed something under the desk. He reached over, pulled a latch, took a small notebook out, and handed it to RJ. Then he continued down the ladder.

When Ricky got to the bottom, he turned on his phone's flashlight to look around. He couldn't believe what he was seeing. Stacks of money and drugs, lots of drugs. He took pictures of everything and started back up. When he got to the top, he saw that RJ's eyes were wide open. He was looking at the notebook and taking pictures of every page.

"Guys, you've been inside 15 minutes. Time to get out of there," Susan said.

When RJ finished, he handed the notebook back to Ricky to return it to the exact spot it had come from. When that was done, they made eye contact and gave each other the thumbs up, indicating they were ready to leave. RJ saw a piece of paper on the floor, so he picked it up and put it in his pocket to look at later.

"We are outside and moving back to the car," Ricky said.

"I hear you," Susan replied.

The two moved to the tree line and knelt again. They listened carefully before retracing their steps to the car. They put their packs in the back seat and got in.

"We are departing and moving back to your location," Ricky said.

"Okay, I'll see you when you get here," Susan said.

As RJ backed out of the tree line, they discussed what they had found.

"What was on the computer?" RJ asked as he took a right out of the parking lot onto Steele Street.

"I took pictures of it all, but it was their inventory list and accounting stuff. You know, accounts payable and all that. It will give us a good list of who their suppliers are. Good catch on the listening devices. How many did you find?" Ricky asked.

"Three. I couldn't believe that notebook you found. It looked like a distribution of money and drugs," RJ said.

"That makes sense because in the hidden compartment was stacks of money and drugs. This is getting deep," Ricky said.

They got back to the condo at 2:30 a.m. Although they got a lot of information and pictures, Ricky wasn't sure they were any closer to finding Riley. Susan went to bed while RJ and Ricky stayed up having a couple of beers as the adrenaline wore off.

They all woke up around 11:00 a.m. and grabbed some coffee before meeting Father Tim for lunch. They left a little early, still tired and trying to process the information from the night before. They decided to get all the pictures to Susan so she could put them up on the board.

When they arrived at the Dog House, they walked toward the back door Tim had told them about. RJ, wearing the same jeans as the night before, reached into his pocket and felt a crumpled piece of paper. He had forgotten about it. He opened it up and read it.

"Does High Rock Lake mean anything to either one of you?" he asked.

"Yeah, it's about 45 minutes south of here. Why?" Susan asked.

"I picked up this piece of paper in the office last night. It's an address at High Rock Lake," RJ said.

"Read it to me and I'll map it," Susan said.

"Guys, there are lake houses and there are lake houses, but this looks more like a compound. Look at this," Susan said, handing her phone to Ricky and RJ.

"What are you guys looking at?" Father Tim asked as he walked up to the table.

Ricky went to the counter to order lunch for everyone, "We'll take four Cheerwines, four dogs loaded, two dogs all the way, a hamburger, and four fries." Ricky said. Then he went back to the table.

"We got a lot of pictures of documents last night and found a hidden compartment," Ricky said, making sure no one was listening or close enough to hear. "In the compartment was a lot of money and drugs. RJ found an address. Look."

Father Tim took the phone from RJ and looked at the house. "That place is huge. It's more like a compound," he said handing the phone back to Susan.

"What do you think?" RJ asked.

"Not sure. It doesn't mean anything yet," Ricky said. He was interrupted by a text message.

"That was Johnny. Because we won the league we go straight to the regional final. We play the winner of Jed's Textiles from Concord and Tommy's Tire Emporium. They will play tomorrow night, and we will play the winner in three days," Ricky said. "Back to what I was saying. RJ, what do you think about keeping an eye on the tire store while we go back to the condo and start going through the stuff from last night?"

"Sounds good. Can one of you give me a ride to get a new rental?" RJ asked.

"I can do it. I go right by there on the way to my uncle's house," Father Tim said.

Before they could continue, lunch arrived.

"It feels good to have something other than a salad sometimes," Susan said.

When the waitress left, they got back to work. "Tim will take RJ to get a car. We will head home and start going through the documents. If nothing happens by the time they close the shop today, come back to the condo and I'll go down there tomorrow," Ricky said.

After lunch they went their separate ways. Father Tim said he would check in for updates, but Ricky and Susan wanted him to enjoy his vacation as much as he could.

A few hours later, RJ parked by Tommy's Tire Emporium and settled in. Around 5:00 p.m. he saw some of Tommy Bonetti's men lock the doors of the store and get into a car. RJ got on the phone.

"Hey man, I'm about to start following two guys that came out of the tire store. I'm pretty sure it is the muscle. Let's keep this line open and see where it goes," RJ said.

Ricky put him on speakerphone so Susan could help to keep it all straight. She got some pins out to mark the map and settled in, not knowing how long this would last.

Ryan pulled out of the tire store and headed toward the lake house. He and Jamie were tired because the last few days had been long and stressful.

"What do you think they will do with the girl?" Ryan asked.

"Not my problem. I'm here to do whatever the boss wants," Jamie said. "How long did it take us to get there the other day?"

"About 45 minutes, but that was late at night. It might take a little longer since everyone is leaving work now," Ryan said.

Jamie fell asleep. Ryan wished he could take a nap, too, but it was his turn to drive. He decided to listen to some music and try to forget about everything. He didn't notice the black SUV that was following them.

An hour later, Jamie and Ryan turned onto the narrow dirt road to the lake house. As they got closer, Ryan rolled down his window and waved at the security cameras. A few minutes later they passed through the gate and parked near where Tommy was waiting for them.

"Just like we thought, we are at High Rock Lake," RJ said over the phone. "They turned down a narrow dirt road. I don't see a sign for the street name, but I'm guessing it's the one on the piece of paper."

RJ made a last-second decision to turn down the same road as the car he was following. He drove slowly as he passed driveways on his right and left. Still going slow, he had an uneasy feeling. Something caught his attention on his left side.

"Guys, they have surveillance cameras watching the road. I might be burned. I'm going to turn around the first chance I get and get out of here. Hold on, I see a couple of houses coming up on my right so I'm going to pull in and pretend like I'm lost," RJ said.

Ricky got up and looked at the map. He needed a place to meet up with RJ. He settled on a spot and waited for RJ's next report.

"I'm near the address that was on the paper. If you look at the map, there are a few houses right before the main mansion. That's where I am right now. I can see a gate with a guard who has a gun. He is trying to hide it, but I can see it on his hip. The fence seems to go all the way to the water. He is looking at me so I'm getting out of here."

RJ pulled out of the small parking area and went back down the road toward the main highway.

"RJ, there is a Hampton Inn up in Lexington. Stay there tonight. I'll meet you in Lexington tomorrow morning around 11:00. Susan and I are deep into the documents we photographed, and I want to finish that before I head your way. Watch your back."

"Got it. I'm heading that way now. See you in the morning," RJ replied.

Chapter 12

"Special Agent Monroe, do you have a minute?" Paul asked.

"Hey Paul. I wanted to talk to you anyway, but you go first. What do you have?" he asked his HRT lead.

"We've been going over the overnight tapes from the target business. Someone was in there last night," he said.

"What could you hear?" Special Agent Monroe asked.

"That's the interesting thing. We don't hear actual conversations on the tapes. The microphones picked up some abnormal noises. I asked the techs to try and clean it up some. Wanted you to know. Did you need something from me?" Paul asked.

"Thanks for the info. Yeah, the other day when Temple and Floyd were here it seemed like you knew them. What can you tell me?" Special Agent Monroe asked.

"I was with them in Tikrit back when I was attached to that Special Operations Task Force. Sometimes I would go on target with the assault guys and arrest the guys they captured or help with evidence. They are just comm guys, not shooters, but I was with them once and we got into a big fire fight. They are good guys. I trust them," Paul said.

"Okay but let's keep an eye on them. This isn't Iraq," Special Agent Monroe said.

Ricky pulled into the parking lot of Lexington BBQ, or The Honeymonk as it is known, just off Highway 64. He parked next to RJ's car and walked inside.

RJ was sitting in a booth in the back, drinking some tea.

"Tell me about this lake house," Ricky said.

"I followed them through Lexington where they got on Highway 8 heading down to High Rock Lake. We went past the Southmont Fire Department and not long after that we took a left turn that took us straight toward the lake. The road got narrower the closer we got to the lake. There were some turnoffs on both sides. After a half a mile or so, I noticed a camera up in a tree. Even though it was getting dark I could see a few more cameras the further we went. So, they know who's approaching. I'm sure they have me on video. There was a turn off on the right, so I took it," RJ said.

"What will you boys have?" the waitress asked, interrupting RJ.

"I'll have the coarse chopped plate with hush puppies and a Cheerwine," Ricky said.

"Make that two," RJ said, smiling at the waitress before continuing. "That turnoff on the right had a few small houses on a short horseshoe parking lot. I pretended to be lost and then got out of there. As I came out, I saw a gate to the big house. It looked like the fence went all the way around to the water's edge. If they are holding Riley there, they have a big advantage with the cameras and that road being so narrow. One way in and one way out."

The waitress brought their food. Ricky ate slowly, thinking through everything RJ had told him.

"This is the best BBQ I've had," RJ said.

"I know. I picked this place on purpose. You said one way in and one way out, but that may not be true," Ricky said. He picked up his phone to call Susan.

"Susan, don't you have a cousin down this way? I remember talking to him at the family Christmas party," Ricky said.

"My cousin Billy has a lake house down there. Don't you remember he took us out on his pontoon boat on the Fourth of July to watch the fireworks?" Susan said.

"Yes, I do remember. Could you call him and see if he is available to take RJ and I out for a boat ride?" he asked.

"Sure. Before we hang up, I have news. I did some research on that lake house. It's owned by a company down in Atlanta but was previously owned by that union Tommy Bonetti was a member of. The title was transferred to the Atlanta company several years ago," Susan said.

"Okay, that's interesting. Now I really want to get out on that lake," Ricky said.

"I'll call Billy and will let you know when I get a hold of him," Susan said. *Click.*

"That's a good idea. I thought of that but didn't know we had a local connection with a boat," RJ said, finishing his Cheerwine. "You said you have something from the documents we took pictures of the other night?"

"Nothing concrete, but something is off. They are paying a lot of money for inventory. When we were there, I didn't see any tire inventory that matched what they were paying for. They use suppliers in New Jersey and Atlanta. They have a payroll of 10 employees, but I only saw two guys in the front and two or three more in the back. Add in the secret compartment under the desk with the money and drugs and the bust on the highway, I'm thinking they are laundering money and distributing drugs. Maybe they are doing it for this crime family that is connected to Tommy's old union or this company in Atlanta," Ricky said.

"That all makes sense to me and would explain the Federal Task Force, too," RJ said. "If you still have Paul's card, I think we might want to keep that handy."

The waitress came back to their table to check on them, "How about some dessert, fellas?" she said.

"I'll have slice of that apple pie and another Cheerwine," Ricky said.

RJ nodded, he wanted the same.

"Good choice. Do you want a scoop of ice cream on top of that?" she asked.

"Is there any other way to eat apple pie?" Ricky said, winking at her.

Susan called just as their pie with ice cream arrived.

"Any luck?" Ricky asked.

"We got lucky. Billy is about to go fishing for the rest of the afternoon. He said it's no problem if you two want to go. I explained to him, without going into detail, that there was a certain part of the lake you wanted to go to and that you would be paying for the gas," she told him.

"Great. Where do we meet him?" he said. He watched his ice cream melt over his pie while RJ dug in.

"He will be at Buddle Creek boat ramp in about 45 minutes. Do you know where that is?" Susan asked.

"No, I'll map it. We will leave here as soon as we finish our pie," Ricky said.

"Pie? Where are you guys?" she asked.

"The Monk," he said.

"Seriously, you went to the Monk without me? Now I'm hungry," Susan said. *Click.*

Ricky laughed but knew he would have to get her some BBQ for later.

After checking the distance to the boat ramp, Ricky said, "We are set. We're going fishing with Susan's cousin Billy. You'll like him, he is very easy-going. We need to be at the boat ramp in 45 minutes, but it looks like it's only about 25 minutes from here, so we have time to enjoy the rest of our lunch."

After lunch, RJ parked his rental car at the hotel, then rode with Ricky to Buddle Creek boat ramp. They arrived a few minutes early and waited.

When Billy arrived, Ricky and RJ walked over to talk.

"Hey Billy, this is my friend RJ. We really appreciate you letting us tag along with you," Ricky said.

"No problem. I'll enjoy having company. Susan said you needed to go to a certain place on the lake. Are you doing some PI work?" Billy asked.

"It's a little over two miles away and close to the Highway 8 bridge. I can show you on the map on my phone. Yes, this will help with a case we are working on. No big deal but sometimes it's better to blend in a little. You know what I mean?" Ricky said. He didn't lie but he knew he couldn't tell him the complete truth.

"Okay, that's fine. One of you jump in the boat. I'll back it down to the water and we will get going," Billy said.

RJ shoved Ricky out of the way and ran over to climb into the boat. He laughed at Ricky standing on the ground having to watch.

"Ryan, get in here," Tommy yelled.

"Yeah boss, what do you need?" Ryan asked. He walked into the kitchen where Tommy was drinking coffee.

"Get the girl and bring her into the office. If she is still crying, give her something to cry about. And bring me some of the cocaine we have stashed here," Tommy said.

Ryan walked through the living room toward the French doors leading out to a patio that overlooked the pool and the lake beyond. Ryan stopped and looked at the view, which was hard to miss since the living room had a wall of windows looking out on the lake.

He walked out the door toward the pool and wished he was out fishing like the guys on the boat he saw near the house. He followed the path to the right toward the garage and the room where they were keeping Riley.

Ryan entered the garage and saw Jamie sitting outside the door. "Boss wants to see her. Is she still crying a lot?" he asked.

"A little," Jamie said. He stood up to unlock the door.

They walked in and found Riley curled up like a ball on the sofa.

"Get up!" Ryan yelled.

Riley screamed, "DON'T TOUCH ME! STOP! I DON'T KNOW ANYTHING! WHY ARE YOU DOING THIS TO ME?"

Ryan slapped her across the face and hit the same spot near her eye that he hit the day before. Riley's cheek was bruised, and her eye was swollen shut.

Jamie untied her. With Ryan on one side and Jamie on the other, Riley stood up.

There was nothing wrong with her legs, so she could walk just fine. When they brought her outside, they wanted it to look like the three of them were simply walking from the garage to the main house.

Outside the sun was bright and Riley had to squint to see through her one good eye. They guided her to the walkway and around the pool before going up the couple of steps toward the French doors.

"I wonder what kind of fish those guys are going for?" Ryan said.

"Who knows. Probably bass or catfish or something," Jamie said.

Ryan opened the door to the main house. They walked Riley through the living room to the office. Jamie opened the door, and they tossed her into the room where Tommy was waiting.

"RJ, are you seeing this?" Ricky said as he put some bait on his hook.

"Yeah. Is that her? No way we are getting this lucky this fast," RJ said.

"Unfortunately, yes that is her," Ricky said.

They now knew where Riley Simms had disappeared to.

"Billy, can we fish here for a little while longer?" Ricky asked.

"I don't know that I call what you two are doing fishing, but yeah, we can stay here for a while. I have all afternoon," Billy said.

Ricky and RJ held their borrowed fishing poles toward the house so they could continue to monitor the situation. They would decide later what, if anything, they could do.

"You are going to tell me what you heard at the bar! Do you understand me?" Tommy yelled at Riley. "Now talk."

"I keep telling you, I didn't hear anything at all. Who are you really?" Riley asked. She soon regretted it when Jamie gave her a harder slap on the face. Blood trickled down her cheek.

"Don't try to be cute with me. You are nobody. I don't care what happens to you, but I assure you none of this will stop until you tell me what I want to know," Tommy said.

Riley sat there and said nothing. She was starting to realize that her chances of getting out of this alive were fading. Tommy was acting like a mad man. She started to cry again.

"What did you hear, and more importantly, who did you tell? Did you tell Temple anything?" Tommy asked. "Your crying is pissing me off. TALK."

"I have nothing to say," Riley managed.

"Who did you talk to? Temple? Johnny Sullivan? The police?"

Riley sobbed louder, which made Tommy even madder. As her sobbing got worse, so did the force of the slaps from Jamie and Ryan.

"Get her out of here. Riley, this isn't over. All you have to do is answer my questions. Your time is running out," Tommy said. He stood up and left the office.

Ryan and Jamie reached under Riley's arms, stood her up, and tried to steady her. Her knees were wobbling. She was scared, beaten up, and hadn't eaten in a couple of days. The two thugs walked her out of the office, back toward the French doors.

"Ricky, look," RJ said.

Ricky looked up from his fishing pole as the doors to the main house opened. The two goons brought Riley out and walked down the stairs toward the pool, the same way they had gone in.

"Did you see that, RJ? Her knees just buckled, they had to grab her before she fell," Ricky said.

"That girl is drunk," Billy said.

"I wish that were true," Ricky said. They watched the trio go into a door on the side of the house. "How often do you get to come out here, Billy?"

"I try to get out at least once a week. It depends on work. It's so nice and peaceful," Billy said. "We've been out here a few hours now. How long do you guys want to stay out?"

"We are done working, but you were so nice to bring us, we can stay as long as you want," Ricky said.

The door of the main house opened again. Tommy Bonetti walked out and dove into the pool. Ricky nudged RJ to ensure he was seeing this, too.

"Well, we aren't catching anything so I think we can head back in," Billy said.

Ricky thought they had caught a lot. He and RJ reeled in their lines and wiped them down as Billy turned the boat back toward the Buddle Creek boat ramp.

As soon as the boat was secured on the trailer, Ricky paid Billy for the gas they used and called Susan to let her know they were done. He would call again when they got back to the hotel in Lexington.

"Paul, come over here!" Special Agent Monroe yelled across the operations center.

Paul stood up to walk over. The tech department guys walked with him.

"Special Agent Monroe, I brought the tech guys with me. They just finished working on the recordings from last night," Paul said. "I'll let them fill you in."

"Sir, we are sure someone was in the office at the location last night. When we isolated the noises Paul heard, we thought it was a few things. The first thing we heard is what we think is someone putting their finger on one of the microphones and rubbing it, almost like they were trying to figure out what it was. The next noise is most likely someone typing on a keyboard. We know that because there is a microphone on the lamp on the desk. The last sounds are intriguing. It sounds like someone is scraping a piece of metal and a door opening but that's as much as we can tell," the FBI tech said.

"Okay, thanks. Get me the written report and a copy of the recording as soon as you can. I want to hear it myself," Special Agent Monroe said, dismissing the techs.

"Someone found our microphones," Paul said.

"Sounds like it. I want to know more about that last part. We need to figure out who it was, too. Any chance it was the PI and his friend?" Special Agent Monroe asked.

"I hadn't thought of that, but it is a possibility. If not, could it have been Tommy or Gina? Or one of their goons snooping around?" Paul offered.

"All good questions," Special Agent Monroe said. "From what I've read and what you have told me about the PI, I think they are more than capable of breaking into that business. We can't have them in our way. We are trying to bring federal charges and bring down the entire Atlanta Crime Syndicate. We simply can't afford to have these two mess it up."

"I agree, sir. Do you want me to have a talk with Ricky and RJ?" Paul asked.

"Let's do that. Let me know if you get anything. And Paul, you can call me Chester," he said.

Before they called Susan, Ricky and RJ sat in the hotel room and talked about their fishing trip.

"Now that we have seen the house from the water, what do you think?" Ricky asked.

"We confirmed the fence goes to the waterline. We confirmed it is the correct location where they are holding your friend. We confirmed Tommy Bonetti is involved. We have our answers, but there is a new question. What do we do?" RJ said.

"I agree with everything you said. I'm going to get her out of there. Are you willing to go with me?" he asked but knew the answer.

"That's a bullshit question and you know it. After seeing that girl and the way she was walking, I have no doubt they are beating her up. I'm in," RJ said.

Ricky's phone rang He held his phone up so RJ could see the caller ID on his phone. It was Paul.

"Hey Paul, what's up? I didn't expect to hear from you so soon," Ricky said.

"After you guys were here the other day, we had some things go on at a location we are surveilling. I'm wondering what, if anything, you two are up to?" Paul asked.

"We are down in Lexington. We went fishing with one of Susan's cousins today. Had a great time out on the water, although we didn't catch anything," he replied.

"Have either of you heard anything new about your friend that is missing?" Paul asked.

Ricky realized this was an official phone call. He had no intention of telling the Feds what they had learned today. At least not yet.

"No, we haven't heard anything from the police about Riley yet," he said. He wasn't lying. "She hasn't shown up anywhere yet, either."

"Okay, give me a call if anything changes," Paul said. *Click.*

"He was fishing for information. I get the feeling he was calling for Chet. They must have something new they are running down," Ricky said. "Back to what we were saying, I don't think we can drive in on that road, at least not the way you described it. That means going in from the lake."

"I think you're right," RJ agreed.

Ricky's phone rang again.

"Hey Susan," Ricky said.

"Hey. I thought you were going to call me back," she said. "How'd everything go today?"

"We actually saw Riley. Tommy's thugs were walking her from one side of the house to the other," Ricky said.

"That's good, right? How did she look?" Susan asked.

"Not great. It was clear they had been working on her. But at least now we know where she is," Ricky said.

"What's next?" she asked.

"RJ and I are going in to get her out," Ricky said.

"Not without me, you aren't. She's my friend too," Susan replied.

"We need all the help we can get. I have a couple of things I need you to do for us. First, can you call Father Tim, tell him what's going on, and ask him if he can help? I have something for him to do after we get her out that is right up his alley. Next, could you find a house on the lake to rent that we can base out of? Lastly, print an overhead shot of the house where they are keeping her. I'm staying here tonight but would like to get to a lake house tomorrow, if possible, so we can plan this out," Ricky said.

"How many days?" she asked.

"Let's say four. What have you been working on?" he asked her.

"I'm still trying to get into her phone. I've locked it out a few times already. I'm slowing down so I don't get it permanently locked out. You know how Apple is," she said.

"I know. I wish I could help but all I know to say is to try and think like her," Ricky said.

"You keep saying that, but I'm not getting anywhere," Susan said. "HOLY CRAP RICKY. I'M IN HER PHONE!" Susan yelled.

"Are you serious? What was her passcode?" he asked.

"Her code is 0130," Susan told him.

"How did you come up with that?" he asked.

"I remembered she's always talking about moving to the Caribbean. She always says she needs to pick one of the thirty islands. I gave it a shot," Susan laughed.

"She told me the same thing a couple of weeks ago, good job. Look around in there and see if you can figure out what's going on," Ricky said. *Click.*

RJ and Ricky went back to talking through possible courses of action to get Riley out of there. Thirty minutes later they were interrupted by another phone call from Susan.

"I just found out why Tommy kidnapped her. This is unbelievable. Honestly, I'm too scared to read this over the phone. All I will say is, her notes app has a lot of details you two need to see. Let's hang up. I'm going to find a house to rent down there and then you need to come home in the morning to see this and get all your gear. We have to get her out soon, she knows a lot," Susan said.

Chapter 13

It was 7:30 a.m. when Ricky and RJ got back to the condo. Ricky carried a bag of pastries they had stopped to get on the way to the kitchen. He grabbed a cup of coffee as he pulled a cinnamon roll out of the bag. Susan was already up and pacing.

"You two read this," Susan said, handing him Riley's phone. RJ stood back and let Ricky read it first.

"This explains a lot," Ricky said. "She's smart. She made notes on what she overheard when they came into the pub," he said. He passed the phone to RJ.

"Wow. We are in some deep stuff with this one. No wonder there is a Federal Task Force in town," RJ said. He read it all again. "Do you think this is accurate, or just big talk in a bar?"

"I guess it's real or they wouldn't have grabbed her," Ricky said. "They probably think she told me everything, which is why they are after me, too."

"We need to go get her," Susan said.

There was a knock at the door. RJ opened the door to find Father Tim standing there. "I hear there have been some developments," Father Tim said.

"Yeah, you could say that. I think we have a better understanding of what we are in the middle of now," RJ said.

"Come on in, Tim, and take a look at this," Ricky said from across the room.

Father Tim sat down to read Riley's phone. Susan came in from the kitchen and handed him coffee and an apple fritter.

"Sorry, the apple fritter is all we have left, but the apples come from the Dalton Orchard near Raleigh," Susan said. "What do you think?"

"I think this explains why they kidnapped her and why they took a shot at Ricky," Father Tim said.

There was another knock at the door. Ricky went over to answer it.

"Who are you?" Ricky said.

"I'm from the homeowner's association. We have not received a response to our lawsuit about the car that has been parked on the street and the littering around it. We would like to avoid going to court," the young lawyer said.

Father Tim said, "I'll take this one." He walked to the front door. "I'm Mr. and Mrs. Temple's attorney. What is all this about littering?" he asked.

"Your clients have been balling up the notices left on the vehicle in question and throwing them on the ground. That is littering," he said. He was confused because Father Tim had his collar on. "You are their attorney?"

"Yes, that's what I just told you. You will be hearing from us. I am preparing a response to your lawsuit, and we will be countersuing for harassment and overstepping your legal rights. I have read the homeowners association bylaws and frankly they read like a second-year law student wrote them," Father Tim said. "If that is all you need, we are in the middle of other business matters. I heard a house down the street painted their door trim without permission so you might want to get on that." Tim closed the door and joined the others in the living room.

After he sat down, Father Tim noticed everyone was staring at him. "What?" he asked.

"We've just never heard you do that before," Susan said.

"I hate homeowners associations. They always push the limits of their actual authority. It's usually a group of people with big egos riding around neighborhoods looking for something to complain about instead of simply living their own lives. Now what are you guys thinking regarding Riley Simms?" he asked.

"We're going to go get her," Ricky said. "We have some planning to do, and there is a role in this for you if you're willing."

"I'm in. There is no telling what they are doing to her and what she has been through," Father Tim said.

"They are keeping her at that house on High Rock Lake," Ricky said. "So, the first thing is getting a house down at the lake to operate out of."

"That's done," Susan said. "I found a house last night. It's about a three-mile drive from where they are keeping Riley. The house is on High Rock Shores Drive. I booked it for four days. When we are done talking, we can go back to the office, and you can see the layout."

"Good. Last night RJ and I developed an equipment list of what we will need. The biggest thing we don't have is a boat. We can talk about that when we get down there," Ricky said.

"A boat?" Father Tim asked.

"Yeah. I drove down the road leading to the target house, and there were several surveillance cameras lining it. They will see us coming and be ready for us long before we ever get to the gate. Ricky and I are going to have to go in from the water," RJ said.

"What about Billy and his boat?" Susan asked.

"He was perfect for reconnaissance, but for what we are going to do we need a boat with some get up and go and someone who has experience with this type of thing," Ricky said. "RJ and I will figure out the boat. Before we go to the lake house, we need to print all those pictures RJ and I took inside Tommy's Tire Emporium. Can you make copies for us, then print the info on Riley's phone? We'll need to box everything up so we can hand it off to the Feds after we get Riley out. We should also make sure her phone is fully charged and put it in a bag to protect it," Ricky said.

"Why not just go ahead and give it all to the Feds now and let them go in and get her?" Susan asked. The reality of what was going on set in.

"That is probably the smartest thing to do, but RJ and I have worked with these types before. First, they will interview us about how we found her. Then they will process the information internally before doing any type of reconnaissance to make sure she is actually there. They will probably send agents to interview Tommy and Gina as well as to the house which will tip their hand. That will give Tommy time to move her. After that they will develop an assault plan. They won't just take our word for it. All that takes time, and we can go get her and be done much quicker," Ricky said. "She is our friend, and we are getting her. If anyone disagrees with me, now is the time to say it."

Before anyone could say anything, Ricky's phone rang. "Hello."

"Mr. Temple, this is Margaret at Dr. Pearce's office. I'm calling because you had an appointment this morning and we haven't seen you yet," she said.

Crap, he thought. "Sorry, Margaret, I need to cancel. I had some work issues come up, and we are about to leave town for a few days," Ricky said.

"Do you want to reschedule?" Margaret asked.

"I do, but I don't know for when. I'll either give you a call or come by. Thanks for the call and sorry for missing the appointment," Ricky said. *Click*.

Ricky was annoyed. "We are trying to do something here that is already stressful, and it's been one thing after another all morning. We need to get to work. I want to be at the lake by midafternoon." He stood up and went into the office.

"I didn't hear you come in last night. What time did you get back from the lake?" Gina asked Tommy.

"Around 10:00 p.m. I took a swim and had dinner down there, then I took some time to think."

"Has she said anything yet?" Gina asked.

"No. Nothing. She just sits there and cries and takes the beatings from the guys.

"Is it possible she really doesn't know anything, and we were wrong about this?" Gina asked.

"I think she overheard a lot. I still see her face when our eyes locked, she was scared. Every time we were at the pub recently, she was hanging around the table. Either way, I think we are running out of time. I have no doubt Johnny Sullivan or Ricky Temple have reported her missing by now. I think we are on borrowed time," Tommy said.

"This entire thing feels like it's about to blow up. Another thing, I heard from Atlanta, and they want this dealt with and behind us. They aren't happy about it. What's your plan?" Gina asked.

"I'm going to take a shower then go to the store like it's any other day. We need to be careful down there. We have no idea what Riley told anybody, so we will follow our plan and continue talking about nothing but tires. After we close tonight or tomorrow morning, I'll go back to the lake house and work on her more. Can you handle the store tomorrow?" Tommy asked.

"Of course, we only have three customer appointments anyway," Gina said.

"Almost forgot, I got a call from the commissioner of the softball league. Since we won the other day, we will play in the regional championship in a couple of days. As luck would have it, we play Sully's Irish Pub for a chance to move on to the final four in Asheville," he said.

"Are we still going to play?" she asked.

"I think we have to. We need to keep doing business as usual. Plus, no one else on the team knows anything about the mess we have going on. So, yeah, I think we play. Who knows, this all might blow over, and we can get back to our usual business," he said.

After putting the Cadillac back in storage, Ricky, Susan, RJ, and Father Tim drove three cars to High Rock Lake. They pulled into their rental house on High Rock Lake Shores at 3:00 p.m. They did a quick walkthrough of the house to determine who would sleep where, and where Susan could set up her office. When everything was decided, they unloaded their equipment.

Susan was busy setting up her computer and monitors when Ricky walked in and gave her some BBQ from the Monk.

"I owed you from the other day," he said, smiling.

"Thanks, I was getting hungry. What about everyone else?" she asked.

"RJ and I stopped on the way down. We bought a lot, so dinner is taken care of," Ricky said.

"Good. Ricky, you'd better be safe when you guys go to get her," Susan said.

"Come on, when aren't I safe?" he winked.

"Well, you were beat up a couple of weeks ago at the doctor's office. And there was that time you got beat up in Asheville. But this time the bad guys have guns. Be careful," she said. She turned to hook up her printer and think about where to put the big board.

"Of course. I'll be fine. Don't worry," Ricky said.

In the living room, RJ stood at the wall of windows looking out on the lake. "How about we go sit out on the dock and figure this thing out?" Ricky said.

The two old Army buddies walked out the door and down the short sidewalk to the dock where the owner of the house had put some chairs. They didn't realize Susan and Father Tim were watching them from the window.

"What do you think?" RJ said after they sat down.

"We need a boat," Ricky replied.

"I agree."

"Hey, what about that guy from..." Ricky started saying.

"He's deployed. His team left last month," RJ said.

"Somalia again?" Ricky asked.

"No, the Philippines," RJ replied.

"I know, what about that guy we worked with that time…"

"He'd be perfect. I was thinking of him, too," RJ said. "I still have his number. I'll give him a call."

RJ walked around the small yard as he talked on the phone.

"You guys here on a vacation?" Ricky heard someone yell from the house next door.

"We are. We'll be here for a few days," Ricky said, "Don't worry, we will be quiet. We have another friend coming down with his boat."

"I hope you have a relaxing vacation. I'll see you around," the voice said.

"What was all that about?" RJ asked as he sat back down.

"Some neighbor being nosy," Ricky said.

"If he only knew," RJ said with a laugh. "We're in luck. Our guy is on leave because he just got home from deployment. I told him what we have going on and what we need. He wants to help but needs to call his Squadron Commander first. He has a boat, the 'Queen Conch,' which is already on a trailer. He said he would call back when he has a definite answer," RJ said.

"So, we wait," Ricky said.

Susan and Tim joined Ricky and RJ on the dock. The four sat together enjoying the peacefulness of a late afternoon on a lake. Ricky told the others about the neighbor, so they were all aware. Until they heard back from their friend with the boat, there was nothing for them to do. Ricky was thinking about another plan in case this one fell through.

It was 4:30 p.m. when RJ's phone rang, "Hey man. What do you have for me?" RJ asked. RJ was on the phone for a few minutes and then hung up.

"He's good. His Squadron Commander gave him the okay. He even said they would cover him if anything went bad. He needs to stop by his headquarters to pick up a couple of things to help us out and then he'll be on his way. He lives right outside the gate so he should be on the road by 5:00. As long as there isn't any bad traffic, he should be here by 10:30 tonight," RJ said.

"Okay, good news. In that case, let's plan on rescuing Riley tomorrow night. That should give him some time to do a dry run and settle in. We will have him drop us off about 50 yards from shore and we will do a short swim in. We go grab her and the primary extraction point will be the dock at the target house. The one Susan has marked on the overhead picture. If we leave here around 2:00 a.m. and it goes smoothly, we should be back by 3:00 a.m.," Ricky said. "Tim, there is something I need your help with. Can you go with me tomorrow afternoon around 2:00?" Ricky asked.

"Sure, I'll be ready," Father Tim said.

After dinner, the four friends went outside to the dock to wait on their boat while watching the sunset.

"You never told us this guy's name," Susan said.

"Right, his name is Ron," Ricky said. At 11:00 p.m., a grey Dodge Ram 1500 RHO pulled into the driveway. Ricky and RJ got up to greet their friend and help with the boat. Fifteen minutes later, Father Tim and Susan were standing there looking at the 30-foot boat with a single 350 horsepower outboard engine. On the back was written 'Queen Conch.'

"Hey man, come over here and meet the rest of the team," Ricky said. "This is my wife, Susan, and our long-time friend, Father Tim Daniels. They will be manning the base here at the house," Ricky said.

"Good to meet you both. I'm Ron. Ricky, I brought a few things. I have some radios I borrowed from the Squadron commo guys, no crypto in them of course, but it should help. I brought some headsets for the op too. I have a couple of other things but let's wait and see if we need them," he said.

"That's awesome. The radios will be a huge help. Let's go ahead and get them inside and hooked up so Susan and Tim can get used to them," Ricky said.

It was midnight when the five of them sat down in the living room of the lake house. Everyone looked tired but there was still a little work to do.

"Susan, you and Tim can go ahead and turn in if you want. RJ and I will fill Ron in on the plan and then we will go to bed too," Ricky said.

For the next 45 minutes the three military friends discussed the plan for the next day and night. After showing Ron all the points of interest on Susan's maps and the key players on her big board, it was decided RJ would go with Ron for a recon ride in the afternoon while Ricky and Tim worked on his diversion angle. Then they headed off to bed.

Everyone was awake by late morning. Susan and Father Tim noticed the boat was already off the trailer, in the water, and docked. They joined the others in the living room for coffee. Susan and Tim walked in to see RJ and Ricky loading magazines with rounds of ammunition as well as three M-4's being cleaned and prepped for the night. Sitting beside each of the military guys was a Glock 9mm.

"Susan, when they take off for the dry run, can you listen on the radio so you can be comfortable with them for later tonight? Oh, sorry, good morning!" Ricky said. "Tim, are you still good to help me? I'd like to leave here around 2:00 so we can be back in time to take a nap before we depart later."

"No problem being on the radio," Susan said. She was getting nervous. This one felt very different than any other time she helped Ricky.

"Sounds good to me," Father Tim said.

At 2:00 p.m. Ricky and Father Tim walked out and stopped to watch as the Queen Conch pulled away from the dock.

"Here's what I'm up to," Ricky said to Tim as they got in the car.

Father Tim dropped Ricky off at the Enterprise Car Rental in Lexington. Once Ricky got another rental car, he and Tim drove back toward the lake. Ricky went south on Highway 8 toward Southmont and Father Tim went in a different direction headed for Buddle Creek boat ramp.

Ricky continued down Highway 8. Just past the Southmont Fire Department he turned left onto the dirt road that leads to the target house. He rolled down his windows so the cameras could see his face.

"JAMIE, GET TOMMY. GET HIM OVER HERE RIGHT NOW," Ryan yelled.

Tommy Bonetti walked in to check out the security monitors.

"WHAT THE HELL IS HE DOING HERE?" he yelled as he watched Ricky Temple driving up the dirt road away from the house. When he was gone, Tommy played the recording back and watched as Ricky drove toward the house, looking into his security cameras. "Who is guarding the girl?" he demanded.

"Some of the new guys you had sent up from home," Jamie said.

All three watched the recording again and were still surprised at what they saw.

"Double the guards on the girl. We need to get her out of here tonight or tomorrow at the latest. I need to figure out where to take her," Tommy said.

Tommy picked up his phone and dialed.

"Gina, it's me. You won't believe this, but Ricky Temple just drove down the entry road to the house. He had the windows down like he wanted us to know it was him."

"What are you going to do?" she asked.

"I doubled security and will plan to get the girl out of here by the morning. Find a place for us to bring her. How the hell did he find us?" Tommy said.

Father Tim watched Ricky pull into the Buddle Creek parking lot towing a boat trailer behind him. Ricky parked in the middle of the parking lot, got out, and walked over to where Tim was parked.

"Do you think this will work?" Tim asked.

"We will find out. If it buys us some time, then it worked," Ricky said.

As they drove back to their rental, Ricky's phone rang.

"Hey Johnny. What's going on?" Ricky said.

"Wanted to let you know the regional championship game is set for tomorrow at 7:00 p.m. Do you think you and Riley will make it?" Johnny asked.

Ricky thought he was looking for an update. "Not sure yet. I should know by midday tomorrow. I would go ahead and plan on Samantha pitching, just in case," Ricky said. "I'll let you know as soon as I can." *Click.*

At 11:00 p.m. everyone was up and getting ready. Departure was moved up to 1:30 a.m. to give them some time to linger near the house and do more reconnaissance. The last thing RJ and Ricky did was place their 9mms, radios, headsets, and ammunition in waterproof pouches. They were ready.

Ricky, RJ, Susan, Father Tim, and Ron stood together at the edge of the dock at 1:25 a.m. Ricky motioned for them to circle up. Susan and Tim edged away and started to walk toward the house.

"Where are you two going? You're as much a part of this team as anyone else," Ricky said. He waited for them to join the circle.

"Okay. Final run through. Until we get back here, I am Grey 01, RJ is Grey 02, Ron is Grey 03, and Susan and Father Tim are Grey Base. If everyone does their job tonight, this will go smoothly and we will be back soon," Ricky said, looking each person in the eye.

He nodded, content everyone was ready. They wrapped their arms around each other and the three military guys said in unison, "Send me."

As they walked back toward the house, Susan asked Father Tim, "Any idea why they said that?"

"I assume it is in reference to the Bible verse Isaiah 6:8," Father Tim said.

Susan and Father Tim continued walking toward the house while the others got on the boat.

Chapter 14

"Grey Base, this is Grey 03," Ron said.

"We hear you, Grey 03," Susan responded.

"We are underway and heading for the target area."

Susan wrote in her log that they were on their way, then moved a pin on the map to represent the Queen Conch. Father Tim gave Susan a cup of hot tea before sitting down to help.

"Ricky, open that box in front of me," Ron said.

Inside the box was a small drone they could use for reconnaissance before they conducted the rescue. Ricky gave Ron a thumbs up, then he got to work making it operational.

Thirty minutes later they were about 150 yards from the target house. They were surprised to see all the outside lights were turned on. Ricky whispered to RJ that he was going to deploy the drone so they could look around. RJ gave him a thumbs up.

Soon, Ricky had the drone airborne and circling the boat. They wanted to ensure they had good video and understand how much noise it made before flying it near the house. When they were comfortable with the drone, Ricky directed it toward the house.

RJ moved closer to Ricky so they could both see the screen as Grey 03 took over as lookout. Ricky guided the drone near the pool on the left side of the house where they had seen Riley being taken a few days earlier. He hovered over the pool looking at the door leading off the pool deck. He then moved to the front of the house and realized they were looking at the garage. RJ nudged Ricky to get his attention and motioned for him to fly it toward the main part of the house. Ricky flew it back to the pool on the lake side and slowly flew the length of the house.

Ricky and RJ didn't like what they saw. They made eye contact, and each held up 10 fingers and then wiggled their right hand, telling each other there were about ten men roaming the grounds. They weren't expecting that many. The last thing they checked was the route from the garage side to the dock, which was their extraction point. They looked at it several times and felt as good as they could about it. Ricky flew the drone back to the boat and recovered it.

"Do you want me to fly overwatch for you guys?" Ron asked.

"I do, but if things go bad you might have to come in fast and I'm not sure you will have time recover it. I think we just have to go," Ricky whispered. "It's time to get wet." RJ nodded in agreement.

Ron slowly moved the boat closer to the rocky shoreline. "This is Grey 03 we are moving in for insertion."

"Roger, we hear you," Susan said.

They edged in closer to the shoreline. When the boat was about 75 yards from shore, Ron turned, so they were parallel to the shoreline. They let the boat settle as they drifted toward the rocks. Ricky and RJ looked at each other, slipped over the edge of the boat, and floated as the boat quietly moved away.

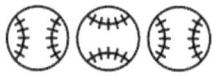

"Ryan, get in here!" Tommy yelled.

"Yeah boss."

"I'm going to be in the security room until we are ready to leave. Make sure people are watching both the front and rear of the house. I have no idea what Temple was up to earlier but be ready for him to come racing down the road," Tommy said. "Gina is back in High Point getting a place ready for us to move the girl to."

"Okay boss. I have a couple of guys in a car at the end of the road with a walkie talkie. If he comes down that road again, we will know well in advance, and they will block it after he enters so he can't get out. Then we'll take care of him for good," Ryan said.

"Good. Let me know if anyone sees or hears anything. We should be out of here in a few hours, but we need to be on alert tonight," Tommy said.

Ricky and RJ were lying on the rocks getting their equipment out of the waterproof bags. Ricky kept watch while RJ prepped his gear before taking over so Ricky could do the same. When they were both ready, Ricky keyed his radio and said, "All stations, this is Grey 01. We are on the rocks and preparing to move."

Everyone acknowledged and then Grey 03 said, "I am at the hold point and standing by for the extraction call."

Ricky took the lead with RJ close behind as he edged his way up the rocks toward the concrete pool deck. Before moving to a clump of trees on their left, they paused to make sure nobody had heard them and to look for security cameras. Ricky and RJ moved to the tree line, careful to stay in the shadows and out of view.

Ricky looked ahead while RJ looked out behind them. He tapped RJ on shoulder to indicate they were moving again and stepped out toward a building that looked like it was used to store equipment and supplies for the pool.

This was where it was going to get tricky. They were about 60 feet from the door they wanted to enter. It was a wide-open space, and it was lit up. There was no place to hide. Ricky saw two men roaming on the other side of the pool, but they were looking at the lake and not in their direction. Again, Ricky tapped RJ on the shoulder and prepared to move to the door. He really hoped it was unlocked.

Ricky broke from cover and sensed RJ close behind him. Although it felt like they were exposed for several minutes, it was only a few seconds before they were at the door. Ricky turned the door handle and was relieved it was unlocked. He slowly opened the door and the two slipped inside. RJ quietly closed the door behind them.

Ricky and RJ surveyed the room and confirmed it to be the garage they saw with the drone. There was a door on the opposite side of the garage, but no guards. Ricky expected to find at least one guard if this is where Riley was being kept. Ricky tapped RJ on the shoulder and pointed at the door. They moved slowly toward it, keeping between a car and the wall on their right side. As they got to the door, they saw a chair where someone had been sitting.

Ricky leaned into RJ and whispered, "I'm going with the master key, just in case there is a guard on the other side."

RJ nodded and then turned to cover the room in case someone entered while Ricky was working on the door.

Ricky took a step back and then tapped RJ on his shoulder to let him know to be ready to enter and clear the room with him. He kicked the door in. They entered the room, Ricky first and RJ just a step behind him.

It was a small room with a sofa on the opposite side. It was empty. Ricky walked to the sofa as RJ covered the door. There was some rope on the sofa, and it was obvious someone had been tied up there.

Ricky keyed his radio and said, "All stations, this is Grey 01. Dry hole in the first room. Grey 03 get the drone back up and see if you see anything to gets us moving." Ricky listened as the others acknowledged his radio call.

Back at the house, Susan and Tim were obviously disappointed as she marked it down in the log.

RJ and Ricky remained in the garage, waiting to hear from Grey 03. They moved to positions that allowed them to cover both doors. RJ covered the door they had entered, and Ricky crouched behind a car to cover the garage door if it should open.

They were getting anxious because they had been in the same spot for too long. RJ felt sure they were about to be found. Finally, Grey 03 came over the radio.

"Drone is over the house. The same guards we saw earlier are still patrolling outside by the pool. Moving to the front of the house."

Tommy reached for his walkie talkie, "Okay, get the car and get the girl. Let's get out of here. Let me know when she is in the car and ready to leave."

After he acknowledged their boss, Ryan told Jamie to get the car, and he would get Riley from the main house. As he walked to the house, Ryan called the car at the end of the driveway. "Guys, we are getting ready to leave. Keep a close watch for Temple."

Jamie walked toward the door on the backside of the garage. The garage door opener was in the car.

"We have activity in the front of the house," Grey 03 reported. "One guy is moving toward the door on the back side of the house, and another one is moving to the main house."

Ricky acknowledged the report and looked over at RJ who was about to have some company. RJ moved beside the door waiting for it to open.

He saw the doorknob turn and the door open. As the figure walked into the garage, RJ grabbed him and put him up against the wall, grabbing his throat so he couldn't yell.

"Where's Riley?" he asked his new prisoner. The only response was the guy shaking his head no.

"I asked you where she is?" RJ asked again, this time applying more pressure to his throat. RJ looked over at Ricky who was still covering the garage door and shrugged. Knowing they were about to be out of time, RJ punched him in the gut and then the face. "Where is Riley? Last chance," he said, reaching for his 9mm.

"Taking her away. Coming from the house now," the guy said.

RJ motioned for Ricky to move over to help. When Ricky got to his partner, RJ whispered what he had been told. Ricky went back to the room where Riley had been kept and got the rope. They tied up their prisoner and taped his mouth shut before moving him to the sofa. When they were done and satisfied their prisoner couldn't warn the others of their presence, they closed the door.

Standing beside the car, Ricky keyed his radio and said, "This is Grey 01, recover the drone when you see us exit the building and get ready to come get us." He listened to Grey 03 to acknowledge before linking back up with RJ to plan.

"I think we wait until they come in here to put her in the car. We knock out the guards, grab her, and leave the same way we came. Thoughts?" Ricky said.

"I think it's the best we can do. It could get dicey when we head for the boat, but there's not much we can do now," RJ responded.

Back at the house, Susan and Tim listened to the radio and wished they would just get her and get out of there. Susan was getting more anxious. Tim tried his best to keep her calm.

The garage door started to open, and Ricky and RJ heard someone yelling about why the car wasn't out already. They crouched behind the car on the opposite side of the door. The person yelled at someone named Jamie. Ricky assumed he was looking for the guy they had tied up in the other room. At the same time, he yelled at Riley to stop crying and squirming.

Ricky looked under the car and saw two people coming his way down the passenger side of the car. One person was pushing the other. He assumed one was Riley, and the other was the guard. Ricky tapped RJ and the shoulder and let him know they were on his side. RJ nodded and waited for Ricky to make his move.

As Ryan opened the rear passenger door, Ricky jumped out and grabbed him, ramming his head into the side of the car. RJ, only a step behind him, had his knife out and stabbed the rear tire. Ricky put the guard on the ground and went to Riley.

Riley was crying uncontrollably. "DON'T TOUCH ME! I TOLD YOU. I DON'T KNOW ANYTHING," she screamed.

"Riley, calm down, it's me," Ricky said. He kept as calm as he could and hoped it would calm her, too.

It wasn't working. Riley's eye was swollen shut. She was bleeding from her eye and the corner of her mouth. "STOP BEATING

ME! LEAVE ME ALONE," she yelled. Tears streamed down her face.

"Riley, listen to my voice. It's Ricky. You know me," Ricky said.

Riley turned toward him and said, "Ricky is that you?"

"Yeah, Riley, it's me. We need to get you out of here. Before we can go, I need to look you over," he said.

"Okay, just get me out of here," she said.

"I see your eye is swollen shut and you have some blood on your face. Can you walk?" Ricky asked.

"I think so," Riley said.

Riley stood up from behind the car.

"All stations, this is Grey 01. Jackpot, we have her. We are preparing to move. Estimated time to the extraction point is about five minutes," Ricky said.

Susan and Father Tim hugged and let out a small yell before acknowledging Ricky's radio call.

"This is Grey 03, copy all. I'm starting my inbound run."

RJ walked over to Ricky and Riley. Ricky briefed RJ on her injuries. They decided RJ would lead them out and Riley would hold on to his belt as a guide, since she couldn't see very well. The three of them moved as quickly as they could to the back door Ricky and RJ had entered a short time ago.

One of the new guards from Atlanta walked into the garage and saw Ryan lying on the ground. The back door was open. He called Tommy to let him know there was an issue.

Tommy reached for his walkie talkie as he ran back into the security room and looked at the monitors. "Temple is here! He is behind the garage," he yelled to his guys. He stared at the screen, watching the three figures emerging from the garage and walking toward the pool.

RJ opened the door leading back outside and looked for more of Tommy's men. He turned to Riley and said, "Get ready. We are going to move very fast for about 60 yards. Ricky is behind you. Just do exactly what we tell you to do. Do you understand?"

Riley nodded, still crying a bit and shaking. RJ made eye contact with Ricky and indicated he was ready to move. RJ turned to Riley and said, "Okay, let's go."

RJ stepped out and moved toward the building that holds the pool supplies. They had almost made it when they started taking gunfire. "Contact left!" RJ yelled at Ricky. They continued to the building with Ricky providing cover fire. He was only a few steps behind RJ and Riley.

"All stations, we are hot. Grey 03, this is a hot extraction. We need you now," Ricky said into his radio.

"Copy, I'm coming in hot," Grey 03 said.

Susan started to panic. She was shaking a bit but knew the best thing she could do was stay calm and do her job. Father Tim got up and paced the room before sitting down and saying a prayer.

"RJ, let's go. The boat is inbound. I can hear it coming in. We need to stay in the trees and then run on the path between the pool and the lake to the dock. I have rear security," Ricky yelled to RJ.

"Roger. Moving," RJ replied.

RJ led the trio to the edge of the trees by the sidewalk that led to the dock. The gunfire had stopped, probably because Tommy's men weren't sure where they were. RJ surveyed the land between where they were and where they needed to go. It was wide open.

"Ricky, you will need to lay down cover fire while we go across. When we get to the trees on the other side, I'll cover you," RJ said.

"Got it," Ricky said back.

Just as they emerged from the tree line, the gunfire started again. Ricky moved around Riley and put her on the ground. He got on top of her to shield her from the bullets. RJ was able to pick off a couple of Tommy's men.

Ricky yelled, "Reloading." When he finished, he got ready to cover their movement.

After a second, RJ yelled, "Reloading. Then moving."

RJ and Riley broke out of the trees and ran as fast as Riley could handle to the other side. RJ placed himself between Riley and the house but kept an arm around her to guide her, moving at her pace. While they were going across, Ricky continued providing cover fire. A few feet from the trees on the other side of the property, Riley went down hard. Someone had left a garden hose out and Riley tripped on it. She fell straight down on her kneecap, shoving it up toward her thigh. RJ picked her up and got her to some cover, then turned to cover Ricky as he came across.

Before Ricky could cross, he needed to reload. He dropped his empty magazine and heard footsteps behind him. He spun around to see one of Tommy's men coming toward him. Ricky pulled out his 9mm, took it off safe, and shot him twice in the chest. After checking the area behind him for others, Ricky put the 9mm back on safe and then back in its holster. He then finished putting a fresh magazine in his M4. When he was sure nobody else was coming up behind him, he gave RJ a quick wave indicating he was about to run.

Ricky ran across as RJ covered him. When he got to the other side, he asked, "What happened to her?"

"She tripped on a hose. Her knee is all screwed up. I'm not sure where her kneecap went. I'm going to have to carry her to the boat," RJ said.

"Okay, we have no choice. I can hear the boat coming in. He's moving fast. Get her ready," Ricky said.

Ricky looked toward the house, and RJ looked toward the dock. RJ yelled to Ricky, "Boat's here! We're moving."

RJ leaned over to Riley and said, "I know you are in pain, but we have to get you out of here. I'm going to carry you the rest of the way. Just a little bit further and you'll be on the boat."

Riley nodded, trying not to scream in pain.

RJ shifted his M4 to his back, then bent down and picked up Riley.

"We're moving!" he yelled.

Ricky took a knee and waited for the gunfire to start up again. RJ and Riley were about halfway down the dock when it started again. Ricky shot back hoping it was enough to get them to the boat.

RJ and Riley reached the end of the dock just as the boat arrived. RJ got Riley onboard and told Grey 03 about her injuries before he

Body

got on the radio. "Grey 01, this is Grey 02, we are onboard and ready to cover you."

Ricky took a quick look around before he ran down the dock toward the boat. About a quarter of the way there, Ricky felt like someone had punched his butt. He was hit and went down. He laid there for a couple of seconds before trying to get up to make it the rest of the way. He was struggling to walk. He heard RJ's cover fire getting closer.

RJ made it to Ricky while shooting toward the house. He grabbed Ricky and dragged him toward the boat. Grey 03 started giving cover fire as well. When they finally made it to the boat. RJ threw Ricky in and yelled, "GO, GO, GO, GO!"

Grey 03 went full throttle and the Queen Conch sped away from the dock. When they were out of range of Tommy's guns, RJ got on the radio. "Base we are heading home, we have two wounded."

"Ryan, make sure there are four guys in that car you have at the end of the road and then tell them to get to that boat ramp. They're in a boat, they have to pull it out somewhere," Tommy said.

"Okay boss," Ryan said. He yelled for the car to head for Buddle Creek boat ramp. "Get there before they do and kill them all!"

Jamie, now free from being tied up, drove as fast as he could. Ten minutes later he pulled into the parking lot and called Tommy. "We are here. The car Temple drove by the house the other day is here with a boat trailer attached. We have them."

The Queen Conch was running wide open with no running lights across High Rock Lake. RJ was on the bow applying pressure to Ricky's wounds and acting as a lookout. There were a lot of house lights on now. He assumed the gunfight woke up a lot of people.

"I can't believe I got shot in the butt," Ricky said.

"If it helps, you got shot in the butt twice," RJ said, laughing. "I'm looking forward to getting you to the house so Susan can be the one tending to your wounds."

"We both know this is a dream come true for you," Ricky said with a slight laugh.

RJ checked on Riley next.

"How are you feeling?" he asked.

"It hurts, but I'm okay for now. Who are you?" she asked.

"Yeah, I guess we were never introduced. I'm RJ Floyd. Ricky and I were in the Army together. I help him out when he needs it. Just lay there and stay calm, it won't be much longer," RJ said. He heard the engines slow down, so he knew they were close to the house.

RJ moved past Ricky and Riley to talk with Ron. "Lots of house lights on around the lake. I think when we get a little closer, we slow down and try to slip into the house without a lot of commotion."

After RJ had left her side, Riley said to Ricky, "I need to tell you something. Do you remember that night you came into the pub, and I told you I was in a bad mood because I had just broken up with my boyfriend?"

"Yeah, that was the night Johnny asked me to help with the team. Why?" Ricky asked.

"Well, that wasn't true. I didn't have a boyfriend. A few hours before you came in, an FBI agent was in the pub. He said the local police told him that Tommy and Gina would come in sometimes. He wanted me to listen to them and let him know what they said," Riley said.

"They recruited you to be an FBI informant? Did you ever call him back?" Ricky asked.

"I was about to call him and tell him what I had heard but hesitated when I heard Tommy and Gina talking about you. That's why I wanted to talk to you after softball practice that night," Riley said.

"Don't worry about any of that now, there will be plenty of time for the FBI later," Ricky said.

The Queen Conch was coming around the bend. RJ saw the boat ramp at the house. There weren't as many lights on near the rental house. A few minutes later they eased the boat into the dock.

"Where's Ricky? Who is hurt?" Susan asked as soon as RJ got off the boat.

"Ricky is fine. He was shot, but he is fine," RJ said.

"Where is he?" she asked. Father Tim stood beside her and tried to calm her down.

"He was hit twice in the right butt cheek. I've been applying pressure most of the way back. He is going to be fine. Riley fell and rammed her knee on the concrete. She will need surgery. Well, they both will," RJ said. "Tim, you know what you need to do. Help me get Riley into the room we set up for her. She is scared and banged up. Her right eye is swollen shut. Susan, after we get Riley inside, we will get Ricky inside and then I will help get the boat on the trailer so Ron can get out of here. The plan is still intact, and we are sticking with it," RJ told the team. "Let's get back to work."

Chapter 15

It took some effort, but RJ and Father Tim got Riley into the house. After she had settled into her room, Susan brought icepacks for her eye and knee.

RJ and Tim then brought Ricky into the house. RJ changed his bloody bandages while Father Tim went to see Riley.

"Hi Riley. I'm Father Tim," he said. He walked in and closed the door.

"I knew it, I'm dying," Riley said.

"No, no not even close. I'm a friend of Ricky and Susan's. They asked me to be here and sit with you while they take care of the next phase of their plan. You are going to be fine, and the important thing is you are safe now," Father Tim said in a very calm voice.

"OH MY GOD. RICKY WAS SHOT. I REMEMBER NOW IT'S COMING BACK TO ME," she yelled.

"Yes, he was shot, but he's fine, I promise you. He was hit twice in his butt," Father Tim said to her. "Please, you need to stay calm. You've been through a very traumatic experience, and I am here if you want to talk about it. I'm going to get more ice for you, but I'll be right back. Do you want some water or anything?"

"Water would be good," she said.

Father Tim went to the kitchen to get more ice. Susan and RJ were there talking.

"How's Ricky?" Father Tim asked.

"He seems okay, but we need to get him to a hospital. RJ wants all the lights off, so it looks like we are asleep. Ron left a couple of minutes ago," Susan said. "The neighbor saw RJ outside and asked about the commotion. He played it off."

"Riley is shaky at best. She was beaten up pretty good, and she remembered Ricky was shot. That got her worked up. Let me know when we are moving to the next part," he said.

RJ told Father Tim and Susan about the conversation Ricky and Riley had on the boat about the FBI recruiting her. When RJ was finished, Father Tim grabbed a couple of bottles of water and went back to Riley. He changed out her icepacks before opening a bottle of water to give her a sip. Riley was crying.

"Are you okay? Why are you crying?" he asked.

"You won't believe what they did for me. When we got outside, they started shooting at us. Ricky put me on the ground and lay on top of me so he would get shot instead of me. I can't believe he did that," Riley said, sobbing.

"Is that when he was shot?" he asked.

"No, that happened later. What happens next?" she asked.

"In a few minutes we are going to call the FBI and let them know you are safe. Are you willing to talk to them and tell them everything you know? Susan was able to get into your phone, and we found your notes. What do you think?" Father Tim asked.

"Hell yes, I will tell them everything I heard and saw. I want them to go down. I realize how big this is going to be, but I hate them for what they did to me," Riley said.

"If it's okay with you, how about we start talking now and I will record it on my phone and take notes? It might be good to do this while it's still fresh in your mind," he said.

"That sounds okay to me," Riley said.

Father Tim got a pad of paper and pen and started recording. Riley started talking and didn't stop for 20 minutes.

When she was done, Father Tim rubbed her hand and said she had done well. He reminded her she was okay and safe from harm.

"No, stay here. I trust you. I can't really see you very well, but I trust you," Riley said.

"I have to talk to Susan and RJ, but I will be right outside the door," he told her.

"Is she going to talk to the Feds?" RJ asked.

"Yes. She is mad and wants to put them all in jail. I got her to start talking and recorded it all. I also took some notes," Father Tim said.

"Good. Let's make the calls we need to make," Ricky said, surprising everyone that he was standing there.

"You need to go lay down. We have this," Susan said.

"Ricky, you can make your call lying down. Once we are done with them, we can regroup. Tim, you stay with Riley and keep her calm," RJ said.

RJ picked up his phone and dialed. "Hey Paul, it's RJ Floyd."

"Can't talk right now. We have some stuff going on," Paul said.

"Let me guess, a gunfight at a High Rock Lake house owned by organized crime?" RJ said.

"I should have known. Talk to me," Paul said.

RJ told the FBI HRT leader the key points of the early morning rescue, and that Ricky was about to call Chet.

"One last thing, Paul, there is grey Ram truck pulling a boat on I-85 North heading for the Virginia Beach area. Can you make sure nothing happens to that truck, and it has clear passage back to the beach?"

"I hear you and can at least guarantee that I will take care of that much. As for everything else, it will be up to Special Agent Monroe, but I will do my best," Paul said.

RJ gave Ricky a thumbs up. It was his turn to make his call.

Ricky picked up his phone and dialed. "Chet, this is Ricky Temple."

"We are very busy, PI, can this wait?" Chet said.

"Actually no, it can't," Ricky said.

"Look, Temple, we have a lot happening and we are trying to figure out what it means," Special Agent Monroe said.

"Fine. At least do this. Paul is standing behind you, turn around and talk to him," Ricky said. *Click.*

"Asshole," Ricky said before turning his attention to everyone. "I don't know what he is going to do."

"Ryan, we've been here almost an hour, and no boat has shown up," Jamie said.

"Damn it. It must be a decoy. On your way back, drive as many roads as you can and let me know if you see any sign of them. I'll talk to Tommy and see what our next move is," Ryan said.

RJ, Susan, and Tim stood outside by the cars. "It's almost time to leave. We all know what we think will happen, but if we get to Highway 8 and there is no contact then we will keep going until it intersects with I-85 South and head for the big hospital in Concord. I will lead in my SUV and have Ricky there with me. Susan, you and Tim will have Riley and the box of our information in with you," RJ said.

"I'M DRIVING RICKY. MY HUSBAND IS LAYING IN THERE BLEEDING WITH TWO BULLETS IN HIM. I CAN'T DO A LOT TO HELP HIM BUT I'M DRIVING HIM!" Susan yelled at RJ.

Several awkward seconds later, Tim said, "RJ, I know you haven't lived in the South for a while but down here we would say she just gave you a word."

RJ laughed. "Yes, she did. I've re-evaluated the plan. Susan, why don't you drive Ricky and the box of information. I'll take Riley and Tim. Remember, once we get going, you stay close to me and don't allow any cars between us. We'll get ready to leave in about twenty minutes. That should give the FBI enough time to decide if they are going to help us," RJ said.

RJ and Father Tim laid the back seats down in both cars so Riley and Ricky could lay flat in their respective cars. Once the two wounded were in the cars, the last thing was to put the box of information the team had collected on the front seat next to Susan.

RJ gave a walkie-talkie to Susan and Tim to use. They were about to take off when Susan said over the radio, "Wait. Hold on a second." RJ watched as she got out of the car and went back to the house to make sure the door was locked. With that done she got back in her car.

"Did you just go check the door?" Ricky said from the back of the Ford Escape.

"Yes, you knew I was going to check it," she said. Susan picked up her radio and said, "Okay, I'm ready."

"Everybody, hold on. Turn off the cars NOW," RJ said into his radio. He got out of his car and walked to the end of the driveway with his gun out. Headlights were coming their way. The car drove slowly past the driveway but didn't stop. RJ took a step out into the road to make sure the car didn't turn around and come back. Once he was sure the car was gone, he got back into his Jeep.

RJ took a breath, adjusted his Nebraska hat and said, "I can't be sure it was Tommy's men, but it sure looked like it was. They are gone. Let's roll."

RJ drove to the end of the driveway and turned left. Susan was close behind him like she was told as they drove the short distance to their next turn. The roads were curvy and a little narrow, so RJ was going slow. Emotions were high and this wasn't the time to get into an accident.

"Okay, here we go Susan. We are about to turn onto Highway 8. Not far after we turn, we should make contact," RJ said over the radio. He didn't hear a response. "Susan are you with me?" he asked.

"I think so. Ricky isn't talking to me. I think he passed out," she said.

"Keep him awake. Play music. LOUD," RJ said.

Susan turned on the radio and turned it up. "Okay, I have the car radio on pretty loud."

RJ and Tim gave each other a look before he said, "Is that Barry Manilow? Play something a little more upbeat," RJ advised.

Susan changed the channel. From the back seat, Ricky said, "Hell yeah, Foo Fighters. 'My Hero.'"

Susan smiled. "He's back with me."

The two cars turned onto Highway 8. RJ saw the Marathon Gas station coming up on the right. His phone rang.

"RJ, this is Paul. I see two small SUV type vehicles turning onto Highway 8. I'm signaling to identify."

"Paul, I see two black Suburbans and one of them just turned their hazard lights on," RJ replied.

"That's us. We have everything set at the amphitheater in Lexington. We are going to take over from here and we are going to speed up. All hell has broken loose on our end, so we need to keep you guys protected."

RJ picked up his radio to talk with Susan, "They are there. We are going to pick up speed after they get in position," he told her.

"Okay, let's go," Susan said.

The two black Suburbans pulled out of the gas station. The front one passed Susan very fast. The second one pulled in behind her and straddled the broken white lane markings ensuring a car coming from behind could not interfere with them. When they were set up, the two black Suburbans turned on their blue and red emergency lights and increased speed.

Susan let Ricky know the FBI was leading them now and it shouldn't be much longer. RJ breathed a bit easier when he heard Paul's voice come across their radios.

"RJ, are you there? Are you using these Motorolas?" he asked.

"Paul, this is RJ. You guessed right, both cars have these so we can all hear you," RJ said.

"I thought you would use some commercial off-the-shelf stuff. Everyone, we are going to speed up. I will let you know when we are about to turn. Is there anything I need to know right now?" Paul said.

"Paul, we have two people injured. The first is a female, about 26 years old with a displaced right kneecap. It's Riley Simms," RJ said.

"I'M NOT 26! I'M 23," Riley yelled from the back of the SUV.

"Paul, I have a correction, she is 23 years old. The second is a 55-year-old male with two gunshot wounds in the right buttock. He is stable. Other than that, we are good," RJ said.

"Understood. We will have ambulances standing by," Paul responded. The other agent got on the radio calling ahead to set up medical assistance.

"You're having a tough night. First it was Susan and now Riley," Father Tim said to RJ laughing.

"No kidding, I've never been good at guessing people's ages. Susan, is everything good back there?"

"I'm good," Susan said, now with Neil Diamond blaring on the radio.

The four-car motorcade raced up Highway 8 and crossed over I-85. After passing Lowes and Walmart, Paul was back on the radio.

"We are coming up on a right-hand turn. We will start to slow down a little bit to make it safe. This turn will put us on South Main Street," Paul said. He looked in the mirrors to make sure all the vehicles made the turn.

"This is the trail vehicle. All vehicles are through the turn and are on South Main Street," they all heard.

The motorcade slowed down as they moved through downtown Lexington. Susan couldn't help but think that she was having fun, she had never done anything like this before.

"We are coming up on our next turn. At 4ᵗʰ Avenue we will turn right again. You will start to see a police presence. The Lexington Police will be blocking some roads," Paul reported.

The motorcade turned into 4ᵗʰ Avenue. Susan saw a police car with its lights on pulling back to block any other access to the road after they had passed through.

"We are pulling into the parking lot behind the amphitheater. Stay in your cars until one of us knocks on the window and asks you to unlock your door," Paul said.

Two ambulances were parked to their right. There were a couple of men with guns on top of the buildings looking out just in case some of Tommy's men had followed them. Susan and RJ brought their cars to a stop and waited.

After a short time, someone tapped Susan's window and told her to unlock all the doors. She did and saw the same thing happening beside her at RJ's car.

Both cars were pretty much surrounded by the FBI. The stretchers from the ambulances had been moved to the rear of each car, ready to take their patients away. Susan walked to the back of the Escape and watched Ricky being put on one gurney and Riley was put on the other.

RJ spoke with Paul and Special Agent Monroe about what would happen next. Susan walked over to join Tim and the others.

As Riley was being loaded into the ambulance, she yelled, "He's coming with me! I trust him!"

One of the agents walked over to Father Tim. "She wants you to go with her until she is more comfortable with us."

Father Tim walked over to the ambulance and climbed in. Riley smiled, reached over, and grabbed his hand. She was shaking.

"Just relax, you are safe now. I will be with you until we get to the emergency room," Father Tim said.

A woman joined them in the back of the ambulance. "Hi Riley, my name is Special Agent Mary Ellen Wincowski. In the front seat is Special Agent Barbara Simpson. We will be with you for the foreseeable future. Just call me Mary Ellen." She turned toward Father Tim and said, "You must be Father Tim. Thanks for all your help. I must ask, is it true that you are a lawyer and a priest?"

"Yes, it's true," Father Tim said as he felt the ambulance start to move.

RJ and Susan stood near the other ambulance. RJ said, "You ride with Ricky, and I will follow in the Jeep. One of the agents is going to bring the Escape to your condo. Paul will lead the ambulance in the Suburban just like they are doing for Riley. They will take her to Concord and Ricky is going to the hospital here in Lexington. He will most likely have to go up to Winston Salem. As soon as they get the box of information from your car, we are leaving."

Susan climbed into the back of the ambulance and looked at Ricky lying there. "I told you to be careful, but you never listen to me," she said.

"I'll be fine. Shall we go?" he said with a slight laugh.

"We shall," Susan said. The doors closed and the ambulance started moving. It had been a long night.

Chapter 16

Tommy and Gina Bonetti sat in the dugout before the regional final. They watched the rest of their team warm up while they kept an eye on the Sully's Irish Pub dugout.

"I still think it was a bad idea to come to the game. After all that shooting last night, someone had to have called the police," Gina said.

"We have no idea what is going on. We don't know if Temple or Riley told the police anything, or if anyone was able to point the police to the lake house. They might just be happy to have Riley back. Plus, sound travels across water in strange ways so we have that going for us. It's best to just act normally. The guys are at the shop shutting it down, so there won't be any trace of what we were up to when they are done. It really doesn't matter now. We are leaving town as soon as the game is over. Did you talk to Atlanta about putting the hacker guys onto Ricky Temple?" Tommy said.

"I did. They said they would take care of it. Do our guys know what time to be here? They should be bringing our bags and everything we need to disappear," she said.

"I told them. Crap! Look, I don't believe it," Tommy said, pointing to the parking lot.

Gina saw a silver Ford Escape with the tailgate up. Ricky Temple slid out the back and used crutches to walk to the field. Neither Tommy nor Gina noticed someone walk up and stand beside their dugout.

"Ricky, I still don't think you should have checked yourself out of the hospital for this," Susan said. "With Father Tim leaving for his family vacation, we don't have enough people to watch everything."

"I'm not missing the regional championship game. I'll be fine. Look, RJ is over there beside the Tommy's Tire Emporium dugout. He has a gun, and I have my gun. They would be stupid to try anything here. It's not over yet," Ricky said.

Ricky walked very slowly to the field and waved to the team. Johnny Sullivan walked over to talk to him.

"What happened to you? Does this mean Riley is okay?" Johnny asked.

"I pulled my hamstring tying my shoe this morning. These things happen when you get older," Ricky said. "As for Riley, I think we might know something later today or tomorrow."

Ricky was tired. They all were. After getting him to the hospital, Susan and RJ were interviewed by Federal Task Force agents while Ricky was getting bullets removed from his butt. After a couple of hours of interviews, the Feds were satisfied. When Ricky was alert, they started in on him. After a couple of hours, they let him sleep. It was 10:00 a.m.

Ricky was upset when he woke up to hear Father Tim had already left for Lake Hartwell. It was the right thing to do, especially since he needed his involvement to be kept quiet. He had been interviewed in Concord while Riley was being looked after by the doctors. The recordings and notes he made of Riley at the lake house were appreciated and were a good starting point for when Riley was ready to talk.

At 4:00 p.m. Ricky announced he was checking himself out of the hospital but would be back after the game. Nobody liked it. After some conversation, Susan drove him to Greensboro from the hospital in Winston-Salem. She only agreed after he and RJ developed a plan to cover each other. Ricky couldn't sit, so he stood with his crutches on the edge of the dugout. A coin flip determined Sully's would be the away team so they would bat first. Just before the game was to start, Johnny called everyone together.

"Regional Championship," he said. "I shouldn't have to say much more than that. Unfortunately, Riley is still out, but we have Samantha here pitching again. Let's win this one for Riley and go to Asheville to win the state championship," Johnny said.

Ricky hobbled his way to his spot at the third base coach's box. Johnny walked over to Ricky and said, "I'm not sure what is going on, but you look like hell. Are you sure you can do this?"

"I'm fine. Like I said it's just a pulled hamstring. Just tell everyone not to hit any foul balls toward me. If I get hit by one, I'm going to be pissed," Ricky said with a laugh.

Samantha walked into the batter's box and looked to Ricky for his usual signals, but Ricky was staring at Tommy and Gina.

There wasn't much of a game. Tommy and Gina paid more attention to Ricky than to their team.

Juice, Gravy, and Woody had a big offensive night, leading Sully's Pub to a 4-0 lead in the top of the third inning. Just as impressive were Otis and Joe B's defense. It didn't hurt that Gina's pitching was off. Everyone could see it.

Over in Sully's dugout, the team was relaxed. They were playing well, and Tommy's Tires were not. They just wanted to get to the seventh inning and end it.

By the top of the sixth, nothing had changed. The staring contest between Ricky and the Bonettis intensified. Chewey and Caldwell scored, making it 6-0. The game was pretty much over.

The bottom of the seventh inning finally came. Tommy's Tires had one last chance to tie or take the lead. They needed a miracle. A diving catch by Otis in left field secured the first out. Samantha was pitching a good game, and she tried to remain calm to get the last two outs. The second out came when Johnny stopped a hard ground ball to shortstop and threw it to Woody at first base. Tommy's Tires were down to their last out. Samantha gathered herself and looked at Juice behind the plate. She wound up and threw her pitch. Swing and miss, strike one. She smiled. The win was close. The Tommy's Tires batter connected with her next pitch and sent a hard-hit ball down the third base line and past a diving Caldwell. Tommy's Tires had a baserunner and a little bit of hope, but it didn't last long. The next pitch was hit to Johnny at shortstop, and he tossed the ball to Gravy at second base for the out. The celebration was on.

Sully's team rushed to the pitcher's mound. They had won the regional champions and were going to Asheville. Ricky hobbled over to his third base coach's box to watch. He couldn't make it all the way out to the pitcher's mound with the rest of the team.

Ricky and RJ saw a commotion in the stands and reached for their guns.

Before RJ could get his gun out, a familiar voice behind him said, "You don't need that. Let us take care of this one for you." It was Paul. "It was a good idea to make the arrest here. We worked on warrants all night and day. Everyone is in place for multiple simultaneous raids that started as soon as this game ended. One more thing, let Ricky know this crime syndicate was into some cybercrimes, and he is on their list." RJ looked over at Ricky. Susan was now standing beside him and an agent stood with them.

It was chaotic at first. Ten fans in the stands stood up and pulled their badges from beneath their shirts and let them hang around their necks for all to see. At the same time, several unmarked cars sped into the parking lot with the last car blocking the entrance so nobody could leave. Federal agents piled out of cars, all wearing their familiar blue nylon jackets with gold letters across the back. They all had their weapons drawn as they approached the field.

The Sully's Pub team was shocked. Some dropped to the ground; others watched in disbelief. Ricky yelled for them all to come toward him and get off the field. Johnny heard him and helped get the team off the field and out of the way.

Special Agent Chester Monroe walked past Ricky and said, "Good job, PI."

Ricky started to give his usual response but was cut off by Chet. "I know, it's private investigator." Chet smiled at Ricky as he walked to the Tommy's Tire Emporium dugout.

"Gina Bonetti, my name is Special Agent Monroe of the FBI. You are under arrest for kidnapping and attempted murder. We are expecting the Grand Jury to deliver indictments for racketeering, drug distribution, money laundering, and cybercrimes. You have the right to remain silent..." he said as he turned her around and cuffed her as he finished reading her rights.

While Special Agent Monroe arrested Gina Bonetti, his partner Special Agent Mitch Johnston arrested Tommy. Other agents searched the Bonettis' car and arrested Jamie and Ryan who showed up just before the raid.

As the agents led Tommy away, he turned toward Ricky. "This isn't over, Temple!" he yelled.

Ricky smiled. "For your sake, you'd better hope it is."

When the team got over to where Ricky and Susan were standing, Johnny Sullivan said, "Ricky, is there anything you would like to tell us?"

"I can't get into all of it, but Riley Simms was kidnapped by Tommy and Gina Bonetti after practice a few days ago. Early this morning she was rescued by Federal Agents at a house down on High Rock Lake. She hurt her knee during the rescue, but she is fine. That's about all I can say now. You will probably learn more as it comes out in the news," Ricky said.

"So, you're telling us Riley was kidnapped and rescued by the Feds, but you show up on crutches with blood soaking through your shorts?" Woody said.

"Yes, that is what I'm telling you," Ricky said.

"Why would they kidnap Riley?" Caldwell asked.

"I can't say. I have to go back to the hospital for my hamstring, but you guys should celebrate the championship. Susan and I will link up with you in Asheville," Ricky said. He turned and hobbled to the car.

The next morning, RJ walked into Ricky's hospital room. It was time for him to go home.

"Thanks for everything, brother," Ricky said.

"You keep life interesting. I have to ask; Were you sore after the op the other night? I think I'm getting old." RJ said.

"Yes, I was sore. I thought it was from getting shot, but it turns out I'm getting old. I'm still going to Asheville to coach the game. Tell

Money we said hello and thanks for letting you come out and play with me again," Ricky said.

"Sure thing," RJ said. He leaned in and gave Ricky a hug. He then turned to Susan and gave her a hug as well. "Take care of that butt of his," he said, laughing.

"RJ, call when you get there," Ricky said.

"Okay dad. Love you brother," RJ said. He walked out to head to the airport for his flight to Nebraska.

"Good afternoon. This is the Greenville-Spartanburg news at noon. A local Greenville house was raided by federal authorities last night. Details after this break," the anchor said.

The news got Father Tim's attention as he was about to walk to the lake.

"A house in Greenville was raided as part of a larger federal investigation that started in High Point, North Carolina. Tommy and Gina Bonetti, owners of a tire store in High Point, were arrested at a softball game and are accused of being members of organized crime. Our sources tell us they kidnapped a girl who the FBI rescued the night before the arrests. Her name has not been released but she was a bartender at a local pub. She overheard the husband and wife talking about their crime dealings and wrote it all down. According to law enforcement, the wife, Gina, was the daughter of the syndicate boss. She was going to take over the entire organization next year. We are working to understand the connection between the house in Greenville and the arrests in North Carolina," the local reporter said.

Father Tim turned off the TV, gathered his things, and walked down the path from the family house to the dock on Lake Hartwell in upstate South Carolina. He set up his chair and set his cooler beside it. He sat down, took a deep breath, and looked out at the peaceful lake. His phone chimed. It was a text from Ricky.

Arrest made. Sully's won, we are going to Asheville, Tim read with a smile.

As he put his phone down, he turned to see his sister Maria staring at her phone.

"Hey Maria, that must be a good book, what are you reading?" he asked. He got no response. "Maria," he said to get her attention.

"Oh sorry, I was reading something," she said to her older brother.

"I know, I was asking what book you are reading," Father Tim said.

"It's not a book. I'm reading some news online. Some crazy stuff happened in High Point," Maria answered.

"I just saw that on the news." Tim said as he opened his cooler and pulled out a Circus Act Brewery stout from Asheville. He took a long sip, and asked "Anything new online?"

"This just came in. Apparently in the early 90's when the northeast started cracking down on all the mob families, the Bellini crime family in New Jersey formed an alliance with the Atlanta Crime Syndicate who was just coming to power. Over the years, Atlanta grew and took control of it all, becoming a major crime syndicate for the entire east coast. There is a little more about the bartender who was rescued. It says she was beaten up by her kidnappers, and she hurt her knee during the rescue. Because of the girl, the Federal Task Force did raids in High Point, Atlanta, Charlotte, Greenville, Athens, and Richmond. They expect to do more raids in New Jersey. That is one brave girl," Maria said.

Father Tim smiled and thought, *you have no idea how brave.*

Tim took another sip of his beer but was interrupted by another text. *Surgery went well. They put my kneecap back where it's supposed to be, LOL. Thanks for everything, Riley.*

Father Tim took a deep breath and looked out at the peaceful lake.

A week later, the Sully's Irish Pub team burst into Mitchell's Sports Bar on Merrimon Avenue in Asheville. It was time to celebrate winning the semifinal, earning them the chance at the state championship the next day.

Ricky and Susan pulled into the parking lot. Susan went around to the passenger side to help Ricky get out of the car. They slowly reached the door of Mitchell's Bar and walked in.

"Kenny King, the man! I am back," Ricky yelled at his favorite bartender.

"Ricky T. is that you?" Kenny yelled back at Ricky.

"It is my friend. Get us the usual."

Before Ricky and Susan reached the bar, Kenny King had a Miller High Life and a glass of Chablis waiting for them.

"What's with the crutches?" Kenny asked.

"It's nothing, I strained my hamstring last week," Ricky said.

"Hey, be careful. Darby Jones is back there with your team. I know you have been dodging her since the last time you were here," Kenny said.

"It's okay. I asked her to come here today," Ricky said. As he turned to join the team, Susan grabbed their drinks and followed him.

"Darby Jones, the lead anchor for WAVL," Ricky said.

"I can't lie. I was surprised to hear from you. My curiosity got the best of me. Why did you want to meet here today?" Darby asked.

"I need a favor. I'm part of the Sully's Irish Pub softball team from High Point. We are in the North Carolina State Coed Softball championship game tomorrow. One of our pitchers got hurt and the other had to go home to work at the bar. We need a pitcher. I know you played some sports in college. What do you say?" he asked.

"Are you serious? The last time I saw you was in this very bar, and you stuck me with your lunch tab. Now you want me to do you a favor?" Darby said.

"Yeah, I think that sums it up," Ricky said.

"I'll make a deal with you. I'll pitch for your team if you give me an interview about what you were doing in Asheville the last time you were here. Deal?" she said. She extended her hand.

"Deal." Ricky shook her hand and then called Johnny over.

"Johnny, this is Darby Jones. She is the anchor for the local TV news. She agreed to pitch for us tomorrow since Samantha had to go home. It's your team, what do you think?" Ricky asked.

"Sounds good. Take her around and introduce her to the team," Johnny said.

Woody came over to Ricky. "Hey Ricky, the blond is hot," he said, "Is she single?"

On championship Sunday in Asheville, Sully's Irish Pub from High Point prepared to face Janet's Pool Hall from Kinston. Sully's was the home team so they would get the last at bat. Ricky and Johnny watched their opponents warm up. It was going to be a close game.

"Tell me the truth, what really happened last week with Riley? You and your friend went and got her, didn't you?" Johnny asked.

Ricky took a long look at Johnny, winked, and limped into the dugout.

Janet's Pool Hall was a very good softball team. They jumped on top of Sully's in the first inning. By the end of the second inning, Janet's Pool Hall led 3-0. Ricky wondered if their luck had run out.

In the bottom of the third, Gravy hit a double deep to center field, scoring Darby. With Gravy on second, Johnny slapped a single between the left and center fielders. Ricky waved Gravy home to pull them within one run.

The score was still 3-2 in the fifth inning. Both teams' offense had stalled. Darby pitched a quick three outs. Johnny paced the dugout as Sully's went up to bat.

Joe B hit a single, scoring Chewey from second. Ricky was being very aggressive, sending almost everyone home. He was testing the other team's outfield arms. At the start of the sixth inning the score was tied, 3-3.

At the bottom of the seventh inning, Ricky hobbled out to his spot at third base with the score still tied at three. Woody led off. He took the first pitch deep and over the head of the right fielder for a stand-up double. He stood on second base, yelling at the dugout to pump up his team. Before Johnny went up to bat, he put Ray in as a pinch runner for Woody. Johnny took the first pitch, a called strike. He didn't waste the second pitch and hit a high pop fly to left field. It was caught.

One out, man on second with Chewey up to bat. The tension was building, and both dugouts stood to cheer on their respective teams. Chewey stepped into the batter's box and took the first pitch. Ball one. He didn't swing at the second pitch either, but it was a strike. Chewey swung at the next pitch, hitting a ground ball to the infield. The second baseman fielded the ball, checked the runner, ensuring he didn't go to third base, then threw Chewey out at first. Sully's was down to their last out with Ray on second.

Caldwell was up next. He walked straight into the batter's box, took a couple of practice swings, and stared down the pitcher. The first pitch was coming, and Caldwell leaned into it. He hit the ball hard between the first and second basemen to the right fielder. Ray took off from second, looking at Ricky for his sign. Ricky didn't hesitate and sent Ray home.

"Dig, Ray. Dig, Ray!" Ricky yelled. Ricky looked for the throw from right field. This is going to be closer than he thought. Caldwell stood on first base watching the play develop. He had done his part. The ball headed for the catcher. Ray slid into home plate. As the dust settled, the umpire stood up and made the call.

Epilogue

One Month Later

Ricky and Susan packed the last few things they needed into their suitcases. They were leaving the next day for their Outer Banks house. Ricky stumbled a little as he walked to his dresser.

"If you would use your cane like they told you to, you wouldn't stumble like that," Susan said.

"The PT lady said I was very strong and didn't need a cane anymore, so I'm not using one," he said.

Susan rolled her eyes. "Are you sure you can handle the drive to the Outer Banks? We don't have to go. We could just stay here and let you rest," Susan offered.

"No, I'm good. I think a change of scenery will help," Ricky said. He got a text on his phone.

"It's Riley. She is at the pub and wants us to drop by," Ricky said.

Susan read the same text on her phone. "That will work," she said and put her phone down.

Ricky got his cane, limped to the front door, and put on his Red Sox hat. Before he left, he got a notification on his phone. It was from his bank. He opened his bank app to see his account was empty.

"That's $40,000 gone and I'm behind on a loan payment. I don't have any loans. What's going on?" Ricky said. "You need to check your account too!" he yelled to Susan who was now walking down the hallway.

"I'm good, my account looks fine," Susan said.

"Could this be Tommy and Gina?" Ricky asked.

"Could be. I'll keep an eye on my account. Did you renew your private investigator license? Remember it's due?" Susan said.

"Let me look at that real quick," Ricky said. He used his phone to go to the North Carolina Private Protective Board site. When he put his information in, he dropped his head.

"There is no record of me having a license. I mean *nothing* comes up," Ricky said, watching Susan go back to the office. "I will deal with this later."

Ricky opened the door and was surprised to see someone standing there.

"What do you want?" Ricky asked.

"I'm here to notify you that the lawsuit brought by the HOA has been dropped. They ask that you no longer park on the street. Have a nice day," the young lady said walked away.

Ricky stared at her as she left, surprised by what she had said. When he got into the car, he tossed his cane into the back seat and waited for Susan.

When Susan got into the car, Ricky told her about the lawsuit being dropped. They drove away relieved as the Dexys Midnight Runners classic, 'Come on Eileen' came on the radio. Ricky sang as loud as he could. Susan was seat dancing. They drove down the road having the time of their lives.

The song ended as they arrived at Sully's Irish Pub. Ricky parked illegally right in front and Susan passed him his cane before getting out.

Riley sat behind the bar with her crutches propped up beside her. Sitting over in the dark corner, at the same table where Gina and Tommy had sat at a couple of months earlier, was Special Agent Mary Ellen Wincowski.

"Susan, do you want your usual?" Riley asked. "And you," she said, pointing at Ricky with a big smile on her face, "Don't start any of your crap with me today. This is my last day, and I don't need any of it."

"Chablis works for me," Susan said.

"I'll take a Miller High Life, the Champagne of Beer," Ricky said.

"Didn't I just tell you not to mess with me today? I had a tough PT session this morning and I'm sore," Riley said. She reached into the beer cooler, pulled out a Miller High Life, and set it in front of Ricky.

"After everything that happened, Johnny is now carrying your beer. He also said you two will never pay for another drink in his pub. I made sure that goes for RJ and Father Tim too," Riley told them.

"Did I hear you say this is your last day?" Susan asked.

"Yep, that's right. I have something to show you, look at this," Riley said. She fumbled around on her phone before turning it around for them to see.

"A flight to St. Croix?" Ricky asked.

"It's a one-way ticket. I'm leaving tomorrow," Riley said. She leaned in to get as close as she could to Ricky and Susan. "This is where the postcards from me will come from. I'm really going to Barbados."

Ricky gave her a confused look.

"Tomorrow morning, Mary Ellen will be on the flight to St. Croix using a passport with her picture and my name, just in case someone is looking for me. At the same time, I will be on an FBI jet going to Barbados. They are still worried those people will come after me. There is a U.S. Embassy in Barbados that already has some FBI guys there. They can keep an eye on me. It works out better anyway. One of my softball teammates from Charlotte is from there and her family owns a few bars. I already have a job," Riley said.

"All of this made me realize there is a big world out there and I want to see some of it and have an adventure. Who knows, I might be back in a year, but I'm going to try," Riley said.

"We are proud of you. You did good and now you are taking your life back," Ricky said.

Riley smiled and wiped a tear away.

"We are going to the Outer Banks tomorrow, so we need to go home and get some rest," Susan said.

"Enjoy yourself down there and when you get into trouble, give us a call," Ricky said.

"Thanks for the vote of confidence," Riley said with a laugh.

Susan turned to leave, but Ricky hesitated. He wanted to get another look at the North Carolina Adult Coed Softball Championship trophy sitting behind the bar. Leaning against the base of the trophy were two pictures. The first was a photo of the team holding the trophy. The second was a photo of the team carrying Ray off the field after he was called safe at home, winning the championship for Sully's Irish Pub. Ricky's favorite thing was the lone jersey hanging behind the trophy. It was hung to show the back side, where above the number 84 it said '3B Coach.' Ricky smiled at his jersey and then turned to leave.

Before they got to the door, Riley yelled, "Ricky, wait!" She hobbled toward him on her crutches. When they met, Riley tossed her crutches to Susan and hugged Ricky hard.

After a moment, Riley looked up at Ricky and said, "I can't believe you came to save me. I'll never forget what you did."

"It's what friends do," Ricky told her.

Riley let go of Ricky and then hugged Susan the same way. "I know how you helped too," she said.

Ricky stood there and watched Riley and Susan hug and cry. The dirt and dust in the pub were making his eyes water.

Riley looked at Ricky and asked, "You won't ever forget me, will you?"

Ricky laughed. "How could I forget you? You are literally a pain in my butt."

Riley laughed, grabbed her crutches, and went back to the bar. Ricky grabbed his cane. As he and Susan opened the door, Riley said, "Hey Ricky, do you know what a hot mess is?"

With a big smile on his face, Ricky said, "I do, and you aren't one."

The next morning, Ricky had one more thing to do before they left for Kill Devil Hills. He grabbed his Red Sox hat and walked to the car.

Twenty minutes later, Ricky stood in front of the medical building. He went through the double glass doors and passed the elevators before stopping. He turned around and limped back to the elevators, got on, and used his cane to press the button for the 2nd floor.

When the doors opened, Ricky walked into Dr. Benjamin F. Pearce's office. He found Margaret behind her desk as usual.

"Ricky, we weren't expecting you today," Margaret said.

Ricky paused, wondering if he heard her right. *Did she just call me Ricky? She never calls me that.*

"I know I don't have an appointment, but was hoping Ben had some time," Ricky said.

"Just give me a second and I'll let him know you are here." Margaret picked up her phone and pressed a few buttons. "Ben, Ricky Temple is here and would like some time with you." She hung up and turned to Ricky.

"Go right in, Ricky."

Ricky walked to the office door, opened it, and saw Ben sitting behind his desk. Ricky limped the rest of the way in and shut the door.

"Ben, I have these dreams that wake me up at night. Can we talk?" Ricky said.

"Have a seat, let's see if we can figure this out," Ben said.

An hour later the office door opened, and Ricky limped over to Margaret's desk.

"I need to make another appointment. My wife and I are leaving for the Outer Banks tomorrow, so can you see if he has any availability in two weeks?" Ricky asked.

"I think he does. I'm glad you are getting some time away, Ricky," she said.

"Okay, what gives? Every other time I've come here you refuse to call me Ricky. What changed?" Ricky asked.

"Everyone in town knows what you did. You don't think we all believe the FBI rescued Riley Simms, do you? Plus, I know a lot of people at the hospitals around here. I know you were in the emergency room in Lexington and now you show up here with a cane and a limp. You did good Ricky, and I'll see you in a couple of weeks," Margaret said.

"You must have me mixed up with someone else, I'm just the third base coach."

www.ingramcontent.com/pod-product-compliance
Lightning Source LLC
Chambersburg PA
CBHW070505260626
47161CB00004B/1468